Mirror Mirror

A Salt Mine Novel

Joseph Browning   Suzi Yee

Text Copyright © 2019 by Joseph Browning and Suzi Yee

Published by Expeditious Retreat Press
Cover by J Caleb Design
Edited by Elizabeth VanZwolle

For information regarding Joseph Browning and Suzi Yee's novels and to subscribe to their mailing list, see their website at https://www.joseph-browning.com

To follow them on Twitter: https://twitter.com/Joseph_Browning

To follow Joseph on Facebook: https://www.facebook.com/joseph.browning.52

To follow Suzi on Facebook: https://www.facebook.com/SuziYeeAuthor/

To follow them on MeWee: https://mewe.com/i/josephbrowning

By Joseph Browning and Suzi Yee

THE SALT MINE NOVELS
Money Hungry
Feeding Frenzy
Ground Rules
Mirror Mirror
Bottom Line
Whip Smart
Rest Assured

Chapter One

Detroit, Michigan, USA
3rd of August, 11:00 p.m. (GMT-4)

"I suppose it's too late to turn back," Jenny yelled over the music as she skirted the edge of the crowd. Mira had assured her they were coming "early" and the place wouldn't be too busy.

"Relax," her younger sister leaned back and shouted. "You look hot as hell. Just strut, like you own the place." Mira took her hand. "I'll give you the tour."

Jenny took as deep of a breath as she could in the scarlet and black damask corset secured around her torso, and followed in her black knee-high leather boots—the only item of clothing that was her own and one of the few concessions Mira made in Jenny's ensemble. She turned sideways to squeeze through the closing gap that had parted for Mira; she caught the shimmer of body glitter on her shoulder under the black light. Their progress stalled at some unseen jam ahead, and Jenny pressed against Mira's pleathered form. "How do you know this place?" she spoke into her ear.

"Remember Jeremy? Two boyfriends back," Mira gave her older sister a reminder. Jenny nodded with a raised eyebrow.

"He was totally into this place."

"Jeremy—the vegan accountant—was a pleather-wearing goth?" Jenny asked incredulously.

"It's always the quiet ones…" Mira smirked. "Let's cut right and get a drink." Like an icebreaker in the North Sea, Mira wedged a path to the bar and ordered the first round. "Okay, ground rules. Tonight is for you to practice, but if you get lucky and want me to disappear, tell me you'll see me at brunch on Sunday…but not before snapping a pic of the dude and sending it my way. If you go missing, I want something to give the police," she added sarcastically.

Jenny gave her a dirty look—she was the last person who needed a public service announcement about predators. "You're not funny," she noted drily.

"Hey, it's been a while since you've put yourself out there; I'm just keeping it real. Safety first," Mira answered solemnly. "Otherwise, you can leave after you've met five new people, reeled someone in on the dance floor, and bought someone you find attractive a drink," Mira laid down the objectives for the evening.

"What if I get someone to buy *me* a drink, does that count?" Jenny posited coyly.

"Definitely! But this one doesn't count," she quickly qualified before raising her glass. "Salud," she toasted. Jenny raised hers and clinked. They inaugurated the night with a shot of tequila, and Jenny caught the flash of Mira's phone as she licked the salt and bit the lime.

"What the hell?" she shouted as she blinked away the momentary blindness from the bright light.

"Pics or it didn't happen! Don't worry, I'll only post the good ones and nothing too racy that will get you in trouble at work," Mira reassured her. "How else will Derrick know just how much he messed up?" She raised her arm up and pulled Jenny into the frame. "Here's one for #Sisters. Give me sultry," she prompted as she posed next to her sister—head tilted, shoulder down, eyes looking up with just a little pout—before snapping a few more in rapid succession.

Though they were sisters, their filial tie spanned nearly ten years between them and things sometimes got lost in translation. Jenny was far from a Luddite, but her cell phone wasn't the center of her daily interactions. It was a tool when it was useful and otherwise an annoyance—something else to keep track of and charged. She didn't feel the need to photograph her food, the few times she'd tried sexting was pre-emojis, and she had found it easier for someone else to take pictures of her instead of selfies when she'd set up her profile on internet dating sites.

Jenny couldn't remember the last time she'd started out the night at 11:00 p.m. That was one of the perks of being in a long-term relationship—you didn't have to do *this* anymore. The makeup, the hair, the heels, the strategic costuming—this skirt was so short that Jenny had to keep reminding herself to bend at the knees, and she was pretty sure she was going to get tired of looking at her own breasts by the end of the night. She caught a glimpse of herself in the mirror; as much as she'd resisted Mira's intervention, she had to admit she did look good.

"Can I buy you ladies a drink?" a suave voice sounded beside them. It was rich and velvety, like the aroma of strong coffee or how an aged tawny port tasted. Jenny turned to track its owner and found herself face-to-face with a very large, very bald man. She wasn't sure how she'd missed his approach considering his attire: a dark green suit pinstriped in a pale yellow, and a saturated dark plum shirt underneath. While the color palette was less than subtle, the quality of the fabric and cut was undeniable. She was stunned for a moment while her ears and her eyes worked out the dissonance, but her sister had no such stupor.

"Aloysius!" Mira exclaimed and leaned in and up to kiss his cheek.

"Mira! How lovely to see you again," he answered in kind, "and with such lovely company." His brown eyes danced over to Jenny. "Aren't you going to introduce me?"

"This is my sister, Jenny. Go easy on her—she's not use to the night life," Mira teased, but there was a fierceness behind the dimples that put Aloysius on notice.

"A special night warrants a special beverage!" He clapped his hands together and rubbed them as he looked past them to the bartender. "A bottle of the finest champagne for the sisters."

The inked man behind the bar nodded and pulled a bottle and two flutes.

"That's very generous of you; won't you join us, Mr...?" Jenny trailed off.

"Hardwick," he answered. "But please, call me Aloysius. I do detest formality, don't you?" There was a mischievous glint in his eyes that made Jenny's cheeks flush a little.

Mira's radar pinged and she motioned for another glass. "How rude of me! Jenny, this is Aloysius Hardwick, owner of 18 is 9." He offered his hand but when Jenny came in to shake it, he rotated it slightly, bent at the waist, and planted a soft kiss on her hand instead. Aloysius was a big man, not just in girth but in height, coming in a few inches above six feet; diminishing himself had produced the desired effect—Jenny was very aware of his presence.

He relinquished her hand and distributed filled glasses to the two women before accepting his own. The stream of bubbles percolating in the pale amber liquid glowed in the black light. "May we get what we want, but never what we deserve." They clinked glasses.

Jenny took a sip of the iced Moët & Chandon served with a strawberry. So *this is Herman Aloysius Hardwick*, she thought. *The man behind the lawyers.* Mira downed her drink without a second thought as the DJ dropped the beat and the dance floor lit up with bodies and limbs akimbo. "You ready to get in there?" Mira challenged.

Fortified with champagne, Jenny psyched herself up and pushed away the last of her reservations with a shimmy of her shoulders. "As ready as I'll ever be." She looked back and tipped her topped-off flute to their host. "Thanks for the drink."

Aloysius bent his head in acknowledgement and gave her a Cheshire grin. "Please, enjoy all that 18 is 9 has to offer."

Mira wormed and wiggled her way through the mass of flesh until they were in the thick of it. She hadn't been sure what to expect when she embarked on this mission. Clearly, it was necessary—better to intervene now before Jenny went full-on cat lady. The discrepancy in their age limited the kinds of activities they did together. There was a lot of brunch or coffee, and evening events were limited to family dinners, the occasional show, or paint and wine nights that usually wrapped up before midnight. Going clubbing with her older sister never really happened.

And it wasn't just their age; Jenny was the responsible one. When shit hit the fan, she was the first person Mira went to for all things: fights with their parents, arguments with friends, school drama—that evolved into work drama over the years—and countless pints of ice cream and wine in a box after a relationship crashed and burned. But if there was one thing Mira understood, it was the need to get back out there when a bastard broke your heart—she had this one down pat.

Mira was pleasantly surprised to discover her sister knew how to let her hair down, figurative and literally. *Get a few drinks in her and strap her into a corset, and she's ready to party,* she marveled at her sister tearing it up on the dance floor. Mira doubted this was her older sister's scene even when she was in her twenties, but no one watching now would guess that. This wasn't Jenny, who owned her own place and had a retirement account; this Jenny knew how to hold her liquor and shake her ass. Mira had to give her sister credit where it was due—the girl had moves.

When the call of nature rang, the long line to the ladies' room was daunting. You could check your hair and makeup with your phone, but they had yet to come up with an app for a small bladder. Mira grabbed Jenny's hand and guided her through a series of hallways and rooms. Jenny noted the number of smiles and nods her little sister got as they made their way deeper into the club, and resolved to ask her about it when both of them had less alcohol in their system.

They ran headlong into a wall of muscle, whose snug black t-shirt was equal parts deterrent and eye candy, depending on guest preference. The tension in his stance lessened at their approach. "Mira, what are you doing here tonight?"

Jenny gave her sister a look. *We are definitely talking about this later.*

Do you want to pee or not? Mira answered back with her eyes before batting them in the general direction of Slab McManmeat. "Just a night out with my sister, but the line to the restroom is killer up top. Think we can slip in and use the toilets down here?"

He looked side-to-side. "Don't tell Scarlet." Mira pantomimed sealing her mouth and throwing away the key, and he opened the door and stepped aside. Jenny followed Mira down the steep stairs lit dimly by recessed lights. The exposed brickwork and soft white light was a welcome change from the manufactured goth-industrial vibe upstairs.

The steps debouched into the middle of a hall, and Mira motioned to the right. The walls were plastered and painted a dark gray-blue with swaths of draped black velvet. "This way," Mira announced in front of a door with a risqué metal plaque—the silhouette of a curvaceous woman standing with one foot on a chair, rolling down her stockings.

They entered the anteroom, a hexagonal room lined with padded benches and plenty of full-length mirrors. In the far corner was the collapsed form of a woman on the floor. Her torso and head rested on a bench and a cascade of auburn curls fanned out and tumbled over the edge. "Poor thing; must have had too much to drink," Mira cooed sympathetically. *Haven't we all been there?*

Something instinctual unsettled Jenny's gut. *She doesn't look right*, she thought, instantly sobering up at the tableau. "Are you all right, ma'am?" her formal cop voice emerged. When there was no answer, she motioned for Mira to stay there while she approached the woman. When the forceful nudge to the shoulder went unanswered, Jenny checked for a pulse.

"Don't touch anything, Mira," she commanded her little sister and pulled out her phone. "Hello, this is Detective Jennifer Cerova, badge number Tango Victor 38256. I have a dead body at the club 18 is 9 in the warehouse district, requesting backup."

Chapter Two

Detroit, Michigan, USA
4th of August, 2:32 a.m. (GMT-4)

"Is this what you are doing on the weekends now, Jen? You should have kicked Derrick to the curb ages ago," Detective Marshall Collins commented as he passed his partner a cup of convenience store coffee.

"Hey Collins, my eyes are up here," Cerova remarked, holding her middle finger up by her face. "Thanks for the pick-me-up. Did you get someone to take Mira home?"

"Yup. Got her statement, and she's on her way with a uniform," he confirmed as they passed under the crime scene tape and into 18 is 9. Collins focused on deliberately not looking within a three-foot radius of Cerova—there were no safe options. "You want to fill me in on what happened here?"

"18 is 9 is goth club central, owned and operated by Herman Aloysius Hardwick. The club comes up clean on drugs and underage drinking, but I'm pretty sure that's just because they've never been caught. Victim is Janice Keller, age thirty-six, works as a librarian and lives in town. She's a frequent visitor to the club and dabbles in their dungeon from time to time, but there were no BDSM events scheduled tonight. I'm having a uniform check to see if she was attending a private engagement," Cerova stated as tactfully as possible. The alabaster statutes gleamed in the black light of the nearly empty dance floor.

"Bouncer at the top of the stairs says she came down alone a little before 1:00 a.m. No one else came downstairs until Mira and I, and we found her in the antechamber of the ladies bathroom at 1:15 a.m. ID and phone were still on the body; no money, credit cards, or jewelry appear to be missing. I've got officers working on getting a list of people who were already downstairs when Keller came down." She tucked away the cocktail napkin that doubled as her notepad as she led the way downstairs.

There was a flurry of activity once they passed through the bathroom door: cameras going off, evidence going into bags, wide brushes dusting the copious prints on the otherwise spotless glass, and the techs from the Wayne County Medical Examiner's office hovering over the body. Collins marveled at the luxury of ladies' restrooms, notwithstanding the corpse; guys got a trough and piss-covered floors, women got antechambers and velvet cushions. "New look, Cerova?" the coroner drily remarked without looking up.

"Not you too, Dougie. I expect that from Collins." Cerova put her hands on hips and cast an exasperated sigh in his general direction. "What can you tell us about the body?"

Adequately chastised, Doug Knoll ran down his initial

impressions. "Liver temp and eye witnesses suggest she died not long before you and your sister found her. Petechial hemorrhaging around the eyes and the blue cast on the lips suggests a lack of oxygen at time of death, but there are no contusions or ligature marks around her neck and I can't see anything lodged in the back of the throat on gross examination."

"Smothering?" Cerova suggested.

"Maybe, but I didn't find any fibers in her nose or mouth, and most people struggle when they are being suffocated," the coroner countered.

"Could she have been unconscious before smothering? Or maybe accidental death—a severe allergic reaction, or she choked on something that dissolved or moved deeper down her windpipe?" Collins inquired.

"I wouldn't bet on anaphylaxis—no hives on her skin, no swelling of the face or tongue. If she'd had a severe enough allergic reaction to shut down her airway, more than likely she would have other physical signs. If she was choking on something, it's possible that object moved further down her esophagus. I don't see any bumps on the head, but we'll get her on the table and do a toxicology screen and see what comes up," he replied.

"What do you make of the fingerprints all over the glass?" Cerova nodded her head toward the full-length mirror covered in black powder traces.

"I suspect they are hers. The highest are here, which would

be about shoulder height for her, and stop at the height of the bench—looks like she was reaching out on the way down. People lose consciousness when their oxygen levels get too low or their carbon dioxide levels too high, and if the situation doesn't correct itself, they end up in the morgue."

All this talk of death by asphyxiation made Cerova's laces feel even tighter. "Unless you have anything else for us, I'd like to move on and wrap this night up. I think I can feel my internal organs shifting around under here."

"No rest for the wicked." Knoll smirked. "We're pretty much done here, just waiting to transport Ms. Keller to the morgue."

"I thought it was no rest for the weary," Cerova challenged his turn of phrase as they made their exit.

"I've heard it both ways," he called out; he always had to have the last word.

"How long does it take to make a list?" Cerova asked rhetorically as she and Collins moved down the hall and found their detained uniform exiting Mistress Scarlet's dressing room. "Are we interrupting you, officer?" she ribbed the newbie.

The young officer fumbled for his notepad and words. "Detectives, I was just coming to find you. I just spoke to Mistress Scarlet, real name Leigh Meyer. She's thirty-five and works as a professional dominatrix for the club's dungeon. She was with clients from midnight to 1:30 a.m.—a married couple celebrating their twenty-fifth wedding anniversary. She knows the victim from her time in the club—both upstairs and downstairs—but she wasn't expecting her this evening. Otherwise, the basement was empty." He retreated after making his report.

Cerova knocked on the door and a silky voice bid her entrance. "Ms. Meyer? I'm Detective Cerova and this is Detective Collins. We'd like to ask you a few follow-up questions," the detective announced to a seemingly empty room until she spied movement from behind a folded screen.

"Certainly," Meyer replied from over the top of the wooden privacy screen, assessing them with a flick of her big brown eyes; Cerova felt well sized up in her sister's getup despite the brief pause. "I'm just getting out of my work clothes. Ask away." The first piece of leather was slung over the top of the screen.

Cerova didn't miss a beat. "You stated that you knew Ms. Keller from the club. What was the nature of your relationship?"

"Janice came to 18 is 9 quite a bit and our spheres would sometimes overlap. She seemed nice enough, but not really my flavor of person."

"Were you friends?" Collins ventured.

Meyer tilted her head in consideration. "I would say more like acquaintances with mutual friends. 18 is 9 is a safe space for people of all stripes who don't belong anywhere else, but we are an eclectic mix. I don't really know much about her outside of the club."

"Was she a client of yours?" Cerova inquired.

"Janice dipped her toes in the water; she came to open-play nights and engaged my services a few times, but she wasn't one of my regulars," she responded as she shed more layers.

"Were you romantically or sexually involved with the victim?" Cerova followed up.

Meyer emerged from behind the screen in a silk robe that came to the floor. The sway of her hips and shoulders was alluring, despite the fact that her body was completely covered. She sat down at a mirrored vanity and undid her hair. "Any contact we had in that arena was in my professional capacity," she stated matter-of-factly.

"Is that a yes or a no?" Collins requested a straight answer.

Raven locks tumbled with the removal of each hairpin. "No," she answered.

"When was the last time you saw Ms. Keller?" Cerova inquired.

Meyer methodically worked a brush through her hair. "Last weekend. It was someone's birthday and they booked the basement for a party."

"Did she seemed troubled or upset at the time?" Collins asked.

"Hard to say…she was getting spanked with a gag in her mouth, but she looked like she was having fun."

Chapter Three

Detroit, Michigan, USA
5th of August, 6:00 a.m. (GMT-4)

The soft morning glow seeped into the room despite the drawn curtains. The gauzy fabric fluttered in the breeze of the cracked window, making faint shadows ripple across the cherry wood sleigh bed. The patter of rain filled the room and a peacock's call woke Teresa Martinez from her slumber. She stretched her long limbs under the sheets, momentarily contemplating the snooze button; a month ago, dawn would have already broke, making sleeping in nearly impossible. The growl of a jaguar roared from her phone, and Martinez's mind fixated on the fact that peacocks and jaguars did not occupy the same real estate naturally. She cursed her stupid brain, flipped back the covers, and turned off the alarm on her phone.

She rolled her shoulders back and twisted her neck and back until she got all the cracks and pops out before knocking out her fitness challenge: twenty burpees, the evil ones with full pushups. Somewhere in the teens, Martinez questioned her life choices, but muscled through anyhow. She headed to the bathroom and caught sight of her reflection in the bathroom mirror between her morning ablutions. Her cheeks were flush from the burst of activity, but she otherwise looked like herself: 5'10", wavy brown hair that came well below her shoulders, large brown eyes with a button nose, and lines that only appeared on her face when she laughed or was deep in thought.

She posed in front of the mirror, pleased with the definition that was forming in her upper body. It had taken some time and willpower, but she had shed the extra weight gained in the transition from the Portland, Oregon FBI regional field office to being an agent of the Salt Mine, a black ops agency tasked with protecting the USA—and the greater world at large—from supernatural threats of all kinds. There was a lot less cardio involved in chasing down the supernatural than Hollywood would have you believe.

Martinez hastened her efforts as the smell of freshly brewed coffee wafted up from the kitchen. She slid the crêpe top over her head before donning slacks and a jacket. Glock 43 secured in her holster, she shut and locked her bedroom window and grabbed her phone before descending. Her muscle memory kicked in as she whirled around the kitchen: loading the slow cooker for dinner, dressing her coffee, making her breakfast protein shake for later consumption, and grabbing her packed lunch from the fridge.

She bid her three ghostly housemates goodbye before leaving the house and stowing her belongings in her black Hellcat. Blue Monday came over the speakers as she fired up the engine, and Martinez mused at how little things had changed from Fats

Domino's time as she drove to work. Traffic from Corktown to Zug Island was light this early, and Martinez pulled up to the guard station as Tessa Marvel, Assistant Director of Acquisitions for Discretion Minerals.

"How was vacation, Georgie?" she politely inquired the familiar face in uniform.

"Fine, except for the sunburn and the poison ivy that got the wife," he replied with a smile, followed by a cringe as his taut sandpaper skin crinkled around the eyes. "You ever been to the Upper Peninsula?"

"Can't say I have," Martinez answered politely.

"God's own country," he spoke fondly. "Better get on your way before I talk your ear off."

Martinez smiled and retrieved her ID badge before driving through the now-open gate into the underground parking complex. Leather bag slung over her shoulder and travel coffee mug in hand, she locked her car and fished out the titanium key from the inner pocket of her bag—without it, the first elevator would only go up. Martinez waited until the elevator was in motion, and then took a quick sip of her coffee before the elevator abruptly stopped its descent. The doors opened to the first floor of the Salt Mine, and sitting opposite the elevator behind a layer of ballistic glass thick enough to stop a grenade was Angela Abrams, half-heartedly flipping through a magazine. A piece of the metal wall slid open, revealing a sizable compartment. "Good morning, Martinez. You know the drill." Her normally cheerful voice was lackluster as it piped in through the old speaker in the top corner of the otherwise barren room.

"Hey Abrams," Martinez greeted her as she placed her bag and weapon into the metal slot that appeared in the wall. "You doing something different with your hair?" She kept her tone light as the wall panel shut and the hum of the scan started.

"Thought I would go blonde for the summer. They say blondes have more fun," Abrams brooded. Martinez hadn't gotten the full story, but she gathered that things were on the outs with Harry.

"Well, it looks great on you," Martinez politely commented.

Abrams perked up a little and looked up from her magazine, buzzing Martinez through the thick door when the scan dinged. "Thanks. Have a nice day."

Martinez approached the pair of elevators and veered left, presenting her palm for the scanner. Once inside, she balanced her possessions to one side for the palm and retinal scan before pressing level five. Through the sparkling walls of the sleek common room furnished in black and white, Martinez walked down the sloped ramp to the door bearing her code name: Lancer. She held her hand to the scanner and nudged the door open with her opposite hip once she heard the lock retract.

She flipped the light switch and her subterranean office filled with full-spectrum light. She shut her door, put her things away, and booted up her computer. When she wasn't out on a mission, she spent most of her work day in her office without the benefit of the internet—which is to say she vacillated between extreme productivity and tedious boredom in her early days, until she became accustomed to the isolation and downloaded a hefty dose of distraction on her tablet at home for when her brain was fried at work and just needed the equivalent of cat videos to reboot itself.

Her mid-century chic office looked much the same as she had left it Friday afternoon except for the new folders sitting in her in basket. She wasn't sure when or how they got delivered, but at the beginning of every work day, there was always a battered manila folder marked OFFICIAL – SM EYES ONLY in black, containing daily intel updates culled from their larger CIA and FBI briefings. However, this morning, there was also a green folder with bright red lettering: AGENT RESTRICTED – SM EYES ONLY.

Her pulse quickened at the implication—a new mission. Martinez tried to keep her gleeful squeal to a minimum as she picked up the bundle of paper. If there was anything Martinez hated, it was boredom.

*****

Martinez sat quietly in the fourth-floor lounge until the towering form of David LaSalle fetched her. Leader's secretary-slash-bodyguard was a wall of muscle that couldn't be hidden behind the cut of his suit. He was only one of Leader's assistants, but he was still the only one Martinez had met. She quickened her pace to match his longer stride into Leader's office, a sparse functional space that mirrored its no-nonsense inhabitant.

"Lancer is here for your 8:30," he informed the petite woman behind the desk. She was dressed casually in khakis, a linen shirt, and a woolen sweater—despite the summer heat, the temperature in the Salt Mine constantly ran cool this deep into the ground.

"Thank you, David," Leader replied reflexively. "Please, take a seat, Lancer." Her short salt-and-pepper hair barely moved as she dismissed her assistant. Leader shuffled files around until she opened the duplicate of what Martinez had in her in basket this morning. After a quick perusal, Leader turned her hawkish gray eyes to Martinez, and the agent could feel the weight of her indomitable will and focus.

"This weekend, Janice Keller was found dead in 18 is 9, a club in the warehouse district frequented by magicians. Ms. Keller is a registered magician with no record, mundane or supernatural. You are tasked to look into her death and see if anything magical was involved."

As was always the case, Martinez had to muster the courage to ask a question—there was something about the small lady before her that made everyone nervous. Her mouth felt suddenly very dry, but she managed to spit out, "It isn't standard practice for the Salt Mine to investigate the death of magic users. What draws your attention to this one?"

"Ms. Keller called in a tip to the Salt Mine within a few hours of her death, and I don't believe in coincidences," Leader replied. "I understand that Chloe and Dot knew the deceased, and she was a regular patron of 18 is 9."

Martinez nodded. "Operational parameters?"

"Keep it low key until you have something. If Ms. Keller was killed, it is possible that someone from the magic community was silencing her before she could inform us of their misdeeds in full. The Salt Mine is a known entity among the practitioners of the arts, but its agents and how it operates is not. That said, Aloysius Hardwick, the owner of 18 is 9, is an asset managed by Fulcrum." Martinez tried to imagine Wilson blending in at a goth/industrial club. She could not.

"Are the police investigating?" Martinez gathered the lay of the land.

"Right now, Detroit PD has jurisdiction and the deceased is in the Wayne County morgue. Should you run into local law enforcement, use your FBI credentials; Ms. Keller was a librarian and assisting with esoteric research for a case. If there is nothing magically untoward about her untimely demise, I see no reason for Special Agent Martinez to officially take on the case," Leader summed up her stance. Her demeanor indicated she was done fielding questions.

"Could I borrow David to grant me access to the librarians to start my investigation?" Martinez petitioned after correctly reading the room.

"Certainly." Leader closed the folder on her desk, signaling the end of their meeting. "Happy hunting, Lancer."

Martinez fully exhaled only after she exited the office and the door was securely closed behind her. Being left alone with Leader was like going to the principal's office as a kid—even when you didn't do anything wrong, it still felt like you were in trouble. LaSalle was sitting at his desk and knew the look well: relief. He had grown accustomed to his boss's disposition, but he had had years of practice.

"Alive to tell the tale?" he joked from behind his desk.

Martinez tapped the side of her nose and replied in her best Mid-Atlantic accent, "Loose lips sink ships."

"A regular Her Girl Friday," LaSalle remarked with a smile.

"I actually need to get started on the sixth floor." Martinez grazed her finger along his desk. "Give me a hand?"

LaSalle sat back and looked up at her. "You aren't going to get very far with just one hand…"

She shrugged. "Emily Post is woefully lacking on the polite way to ask to borrow an eyeball."

He chuckled as he stood and escorted her to the elevators. After his palm and retinal scans were accepted, he pressed the button for the sixth floor. "Say hi to the twins for me."

Martinez smiled and called back, "Will do. Thanks!" before the elevator doors closed. LaSalle returned to his desk and shook his head. *Her code name should have been Trouble.* He unlocked his station and prepared for Leader's next appointment.

*****

Martinez wound through the saline hallways of the sixth floor until she reached the central desk, the typical perch of Chloe and Dot, the conjoined twins that resided over the numerous tomes collected by the Salt Mine. This morning, the desk was uncharacteristically empty, but it didn't take long for Martinez to suss them out among the stacks. All sisters fought, but being literally joined at the hip seemed to spur greater debate between the disparate librarians.

"Chloe, Dot…it's Martinez," she announced herself.

A blonde head popped out from a row of the stacks. "Oh, hello! We weren't expecting you this morning," Chloe greeted her.

"I just came down to ask you a few questions about Janice Keller," Martinez explained. "I understand you knew her socially?"

Chloe's cheerful smile dropped. "It's a shame about Janice. Why don't you take a seat at the desk; we're almost done here. Help yourself to some water while you wait."

Martinez doubled back and got comfortable with a drink—Chloe's concept of time could be a little fuzzy. If Dot had told her they were almost done, it would be less than five minutes, tops. She ran her fingers and eyes over the spines stacked on the desk: *Creatures of Ancient Persia, Deities of Mesopotamia, Treatises on I Ching, The Unseen Hand, Psalms of the Dead.* She marveled at the sheer amount of knowledge the twins must have between them with their eidetic memories.

"Didn't we give you enough reading during your training?" Dot ribbed Martinez as they took their seat behind the desk.

"You never know when you're going to need a good song of the dead," Martinez quipped back. Dot smirked approvingly.

"I take it you are assigned to look into Janice Keller's death?" Chloe brought the conversation back on track.

"Yes. Any insight into her life and magical predilections would be helpful." Martinez pulled out a notepad from her inner pocket.

"Well, she was a librarian—at a mundane library, not like us," Chloe qualified. "She had been in the area for almost twenty years—a runaway Aloysius took in until she legally became an adult. He helped her get her life back on track and taught her how to not kill herself with magic."

"It was more performance than magic," Dot scoffed.

Chloe would have kicked her sister, if only she wouldn't have felt it too. "Really, Dot? Speaking ill of the dead—that's low even for you. She was our friend."

"No, she was your friend," Dot clarified. "I was merely subject to her company from time to time. She was another nutty magician who played with forces she didn't understand, and I don't believe in sanitizing the narrative just because someone has died."

"What do you mean by 'nutty'?" Martinez struck while the iron was hot—she had worked enough with Dot to know when she was whipping herself into a good grumble.

"Janice fancied herself a diviner of sorts, very into using mirrors and reflective surfaces in her practice," Chloe answered diplomatically.

"She liked her own reflection," Dot countered. "And don't forget all the goddess woo-woo."

Chloe bit her lip. "Okay, I'll give you that one." Dot beamed at her victory.

"Goddess woo-woo?" Martinez interjected.

"Everyone processes how to use magic differently," Chloe prefaced. "And Janice understood magic through evoking the goddess."

"So she was Wiccan?" Martinez guessed.

"Janice wasn't disciplined enough to commit to being Wiccan," Dot retorted. "She sort of made up her own hodgepodge scheme and attributed it to a female creator deity who she saw in any culture that suited her."

"Janice considered herself 'pan-spiritual'," Chloe interjected euphemistically.

"She was like a little kid chasing butterflies, flittering after whatever crossed her path or was currently trending. Crystals, smudging, auras, essential oils, voodoo, Ayurveda, aligning chakras, unblocking and channeling chi—you name it, she probably dabbled in it," Dot rattled off. "Remember when she tried blood magic and saved her menstrual blood to 'enhance' her potions?"

Chloe shivered. "I never was able to accept another drink or morsel of food from her after that phase."

"The most frustrating thing was that she actually made some of it work! Most of it was bunk, but just enough panned out to encourage her to keep experimenting, which just gives all practitioners of the arts a bad name," Dot harrumphed.

"So, she was into all the kooky trappings, but genuinely so?" Martinez tread carefully.

"Precisely," the twins uncharacteristically answered in unison.

"For someone not professionally trained, she wasn't all bad with divination and scrying," Chloe gave her credit. "She predicted the attempt to raise Dagoth."

"She saw a giant phallus rising out of a white mist in her crystal ball," Dot said flatly.

"She used a crystal ball?" Martinez asked dubiously.

Dot shot her a look. "Exactly."

"What about when one of her tips helped Aurora banish that oni?"

"Making vague statements that could be interpreted into what happened after the fact isn't the same as being right using divination," Dot posited.

"Such is the nature of looking into the future," Chloe

argued. "It's not like looking into the past that has already happened. There are many possible futures, and you have to ride a fine line between focusing on specifics and what is more likely to happen. It's sort of the Heisenberg uncertainty principle of divination," she explained for Martinez's benefit. She looked at Dot. "But I never heard you turn down one of her stock tips," she needled.

Martinez cast a condescending glance to the surlier of the twins. "What?"

Dot pushed back. "It's not insider trading if you use divination…and in our line of work, a nest egg is essential to living a long life. You never know when you will have to burn a lot of karma quick."

Martinez shifted gears, refusing to get dragged deeper into what was clearly a long-standing debate. "What about her personal life? Her file said no family or roommates, but do you know if she seeing anyone?"

"Nothing more than the flavor of the month." Chloe shrugged. "She generally preferred women, but dropped in the occasional lad to keep things interesting."

"Any enemies in the magic community?" Martinez probed.

"Not that I know of," Chloe responded and looked to Dot.

"Janice was an odd bird, but a friendly one that got along with everyone. I don't know of any old grudges or axes to grind," she confirmed her sister's impression.

"When was the last time you guys saw her alive?"

"Last week. One of our mutual friends was having a birthday party at 18 is 9," Chloe replied.

"And did she seem out of sorts or troubled?"

"She was excited about some mirror she bought online… something old and Persian?" Chloe offered.

Dot rolled her eyes. The fact that Chloe couldn't remember indicated how much she hadn't been paying attention. "It was Persian."

Martinez kept her composure; the twins were in full form today. "Did either of you know she called in a tip to the Salt Mine a few hours before she was found dead?"

They both perked up. "And she left her name?" Chloe asked.

"As far as I know, yes. Is that odd?" Martinez replied.

Chloe frowned. "A little. Most of those tips reporting questionable magical practice are made anonymously—"

"No one likes a narc," Dot interjected.

"—and if something supernaturally nasty is going down, the tip line usually isn't the first we're hearing about it, but there can be an uptick in calls." The hotline was little more than a number a practitioner could call and leave a message; there was no greeting to identify it as the Salt Mine should it accidentally get dialed by a non-magician.

Dot came out of her fit of pique. "What was the message she left?"

Martinez flipped through her file. "The Hollow has arrived."

Chapter Four

Detroit, Michigan, USA
5th of August, 9:45 a.m. (GMT-4)

Doug Knoll was finishing his last pass when he heard the double doors open behind him. "Doug, someone here to see you about Janice Keller," one of his associates called out.

Knoll pulled both ends of the thread and clipped the excess—even though his patients were no longer among the living, that didn't excuse sloppy work in his mind. "Cerova, I'm literally putting in the last stitch. At least give a guy a coffee break before busting in for a cause of death," he chided without looking up.

He heard someone clearing their throat and raised his eyes to the tall Latina standing in front of him and flashing her badge. "I'm Special Agent Martinez of the FBI. I understand you performed the autopsy on Janice Keller. I would like to ask you a few questions, if you have the time." Under the guise of examining her identification, he gave her the once over: trim, serious, definitely carrying concealed, and pretty. Her eyes were the color of a stirred cappuccino, and her wavy brown hair was tied back, with little wisps that escaped her bobby pins.

"My apologies, Special Agent Martinez. I thought you

were one of my venerable colleagues in the Detroit PD." He deposited the needles and scissors in the sharps container, tossing the soiled material into the biohazard bin. "I'm Doug Knoll, the medical examiner, and I've just finished with Ms. Keller."

"May I take a look?" she asked, grabbing a pair of clean gloves from the box on the wall.

Her enthusiasm caught him off guard—most detectives just wanted the links but weren't really interested in how the sausage was made. Knoll tilted his head deferentially. "Be my guest."

Martinez looked over the mortal remains of Janice Keller, with her T-incision neatly sewn up. "Have you ascertained a cause of death?"

"Asphyxia, mechanism unknown," he answered simply.

"What exactly do you mean by that?" Martinez inquired.

"It means this one is weird. She has all the physical hallmarks of death by hypoxia—note the petechial hemorrhaging and the periorbital cyanosis." He leaned in over the body, not quite touching Martinez but close enough to get a whiff of honeysuckle and almond emanating from her. "But there are no ligatures, contusions, or bruises on the body...well, except for the old ones on her tush."

Martinez gave him a bemused smirk—medical terminology was fine except for tushes? "Consistent with her extracurricular activities, I gather," she tactfully filled in the blanks from what she'd read in her briefing on the deceased.

Knoll was intrigued with just how much she seemed to know about the deceased. "Can I ask what interest the FBI has in her death?"

"She was assisting us in one of our ongoing investigations," she answered broadly. "Naturally, her demise attracted our attention. If you tell me it's by natural causes and there's nothing to see here, then my curiosity is sated," Martinez bluffed.

"Would that were the case," Knoll responded. "When I opened her up, things got even stranger. If someone is strangled or suffocated, you usually see signs of high intravascular pressure in the organs, but the damage in hers didn't exhibit that. If anything, it looks like her blood pressure dropped precipitously, even though she didn't have any blood loss."

Martinez's forehead wrinkled. "Hypothetically speaking, what conditions could cause that?"

Knoll mentally noted that she added the qualifier for him—this wasn't her first tango with an ME. "It's going to sound crazy," he warned her.

"Trust me, I've probably seen crazier," she replied flatly.

"It's almost like the breath was sucked out of her, like she was thrown into a vacuum—not the Hoover kind that scares dogs, but the deep-space kind. The change in pressure causes the gas exchange to reverse: oxygen gets pulled out of the body and deposited back into the lungs to escape the body during exhalation. She would have lost consciousness pretty quick—

maybe fifteen or twenty seconds? But if the conditions didn't change, death would be a certainty in under two minutes."

One of her eyebrows raised. "How did you put all this together? I'm guessing Wayne County doesn't have too many deaths by vacuum."

Knoll paused and blushed a little. "Science fiction enthusiast. You can't imagine the uproar and debate online among science nerds when Hollywood gets space wrong."

Martinez shrugged nonchalantly. "In space, no one can hear you scream." Knoll had never had a woman cite *Alien* to him before; he kinda liked it. "Did you find anything else odd?"

Knoll composed himself. "Well, there was this in her lungs." He held up a specimen cup. "It's too thick and stringy for normal respiratory mucosal secretions, and her lungs didn't look like a smoker's. I was going to send it out for further analysis."

"Was she drugged?"

"Initial tox screen was negative, and her blood alcohol wasn't anything to write home about," he answered.

"Would you mind sending me a copy of the report when you finish it and get the results back from the substance in the lungs?" Martinez patted down her pockets, feigning frustration. "Sorry, I'm all out of cards. Maybe we can go to your office and exchange information?"

"Sounds good to me," he responded. "Just let me put Ms.

Keller to bed." He pulled the sheet over the body and carefully put her back into her slot in chilled storage before removing his gloves and washing up. "If you'll just follow me."

Martinez made idle conversation with Knoll on the short stroll away from the morgue. She'd practiced the art of conversing without saying anything, making people feel like they really knew her without actually having any concrete facts about her. She waited until they were inside his office and he was solidly into his e-mail before she affected surprise—she must have left her phone in the morgue!

She banked on him having a ton of e-mail in his inbox on a Monday morning and artfully apologized for her absentmindedness—no, he should stay and take care of his work; she would just pop in and grab her phone on her way out. Once she was back inside the morgue, Martinez pulled Keller out and dusted the sheet with a puff of fine salt from her vape pen saltcaster. She snapped a picture of the signature that appeared before ruffling the fabric; their magic spent, the minuscule white grains fell to the floor.

Martinez pulled a small pair of scissors and a plastic bag from her pocket, clipping a little of Keller's fiery curls. If she'd learned anything training with Wilson, it was the fact that you never knew when you might need a little bit of someone's hair for later.

*****

After speaking with the ME, Martinez had little doubt something hinky had happened. The only magical signature on Keller's body was her own, which Martinez had from her briefing. Presuming that her death by vacuum didn't occur naturally, Martinez was left with few alternatives: Keller killed herself with magic, someone killed her without using magic, someone used magic but had already scrubbed their signature, or the ever-possible wildcard—something supernatural she hadn't heard of.

Martinez mentally made a to-do list and placed tasks in the correct order of operations. Eventually, Special Agent Martinez was going to have to make inquiries to get more information about the scene of the crime and to gain access to Keller's personal possessions at the time of death, but not before she had a private peek at Keller's home. With any luck, Detroit PD hadn't been through it yet.

It was a short drive from the Wayne County Medical Examiner's Office to Janice Keller's home in University District. The picturesque homes with manicured lawns were a far cry from the depictions of urban blight for which Detroit had become renowned. Martinez pulled up to a beautiful two-story Tudor-style home with decorative half-timber over crosshatched yellow brickwork. The pale stonework framing the windows was accented by dark casements with proud lintels and sills. A recently trimmed low hedge bordered the front of the bay windows on the ground floor. She double-checked the address to make sure she had the right house; it was hardly what she'd expected on a librarian's salary.

A walk around the property and a quick glance through the windows revealed no security system or signs of activity within. Additionally, Martinez saw no fluttering curtains or nosy neighbors conspicuously working in the yard; everyone that lived in this neighborhood was at work or going about their business at this time of day. She slipped to the back door and put on a pair of thin gloves. Fishing out her lock pick card, she popped out the necessary tools for the mechanism in front of her and dexterously wiggled the bits until the lock gave way.

Once inside, Martinez took stock of her surroundings. The decor was eclectic, like an import-export company had set up shop inside. The first thing she noticed was the magical defenses in place. A thin line of red brick dust lined the doors and windowsills, demarcating a line of protection within the home that none with ill intent could pass. Hanging in the bay window was a convex feng shui bagua mirror set in an octagonal polished brass piece engraved with Chinese characters, designed to repel negative energy, attract positivity, and improve the flow of chi through the house. Just inside the front door on the right side at about shoulder height was a mezuzah with Hebrew script, protecting the abode by repelling evil.

Given the mishmash of talismans, Martinez wondered if there were other unseen measures established. She wasn't expecting much, certainly nothing compared to the security she had at her place. Granted, Wilson had set it up initially for himself, and his extreme caution coupled with the knowledge available to him via the Salt Mine gave him a leg up over the standard practitioner. Martinez simply had the good fortune of inheriting it. She'd had a crash course in protective magic once he'd passed all the ritual responsibilities to her after she'd become accustomed to using magic a few months ago.

Martinez focused her will to see what protections were active—*Hail Mary, full of grace...* She opened her eyes to a generic low-level ward against evil creatures and malignant forces. It would be enough to keep out the riffraff, but not enough to stop a determined will. Martinez scanned the front door and found an oddly robust ward specifically against devils. *Oh Janice, what have you been getting into?* she thought to herself as she embarked on a systematic search for Keller's magic room, saltcaster on the ready.

The ground floor held a mudroom, kitchen, dining room, and a spacious living room with the inviting bay window. Besides a hefty mortar and pestle and a vast collection of components for blending and brewing concoctions, nothing seemed out of the ordinary. Hidden behind a plain door coming off the kitchen was a set of stairs down to an unfinished basement housing all the mechanicals, electrics, and plumbing—no esoteric lair there. In the center of the house was a more prominent flight of stairs leading up to the second story, but Martinez turned her attention to the door tucked into the dark corner on the other side of the stairwell. A flip of the light switch illuminated the small powder room with a small sink and toilet, but the oval mirror on the wall was covered with a black cloth. Martinez swept the fabric aside to inspect the beveled glass set in its gilded frame, but found nothing untoward. She left everything as it was, turned off the light, and moved upstairs.

On the landing stood a series of short pillars displaying various items: a Mayan stone fertility goddess that was mostly a swollen belly with breasts and thighs, a red on black Grecian vessel of Artemis on the hunt, and another fertility statue carved out of burl wood with pendulous breasts and an elongated face. Four Hindu goddesses hung on the wall between them, stylized paintings on silk. Dressed in white, Saraswati sat in a blooming white lotus holding a long stringed instrument in two of her four arms, while her others held a book and a marigold garland. The eight-armed Durga radiated calm serenity in her face despite the impressive array of weapons she held in each hand. Also sitting within a lotus, Lakshmi wore flowing red embroidered with golden thread holding pink lotuses in two of her hands while elephants bearing brass water pots in their trunks bookended her, symbolically poured blessings upon her. On the far end stood Kali, a blue goddess wearing a garland of heads and belt of arms. Her palms were stained red, one welding a bloody curved sword and another a severed head. Her left foot was firmly planted on her consort Shiva. Martinez was starting to see what the twins meant by pan-spiritual goddess worship.

The landing split into two directions, and Martinez stuck to the right, walking past Kali's crimson eyes and lolling tongue. The first door opened to a study with an antique writing desk facing out the curtained window. A closed laptop graced the top, with a stream of cords tucked behind and to the side. Martinez opened the drawers and found the usual collage of clutter: post-its, pens, pencils, fasteners, erasers, rubber bands, and little knickknacks whose value was purely sentimental. She checked for false bottoms, hidden compartments, and things tucked under the drawers themselves, but found nothing.

She perused the bookshelves lining one wall; their slats bowed slightly under the weight of their contents. There was a mix of titles across a wide range of topics, and the section dedicated to occult, religious studies, and ethnographic exploration of magic systems all looked like secondary works. Besides a few collectors' editions of fiction and poetry, none of the books looked older than mid-twentieth century. Martinez stepped back, looking for something out-of-place or a title that seemed preferentially selected, but nothing caught her eye and a layer dust was uniformly deposited across the front of the books.

The next room was the master bedroom. Martinez didn't recognize the signature on the paintings, but they made Georgia O'Keefe's work seem downright prudish. The en-suite bathroom resembled a roman bathhouse with colorful mosaics on the walls and floor, and the only mirror in the room was covered, this time with a large bath sheet. She made quick work and found all the usual hiding spots: a stash of extra cash, the good jewelry, the lube and toys, but nothing that registered a magical signature. She had two more puffs before she needed to reload her saltcaster and three more doors to explore.

Martinez backtracked to the landing and opened the first door just past a fertility figure: a guest bedroom buried underneath craft supplies. A loom took up much of the space, with colorful threads set up for the warp and the shuttle loaded to lay down the weft. The handful of colorful sketches were the only hints of what Keller had in mind for her otherwise blank textile slate. One looked Egyptian in design and palette, two looked Chinese with different figures in each, and one was a striking nude by the water.

The next door was a full bathroom whose vast mounted wall mirror was covered with a painter's drop cloth hammered into place. As she moved on to the final door, Martinez recited the aphorism her older sister had said many a time to her— *twice is a coincidence, three times is a pattern.*

Martinez had a good feeling about this room. Unlike the other doors, this one was locked, only a minor inconvenience to Martinez and her lock picks. A woody, slightly pungent aroma with a sweet finish hit Martinez as she opened the door. The light from the landing flooded the first few feet but tapered into the blackness that otherwise filled the room. Martinez found the light switch, which gave the room a hazy glow. Unlike the other rooms in the house, the windows were covered with light-blocking curtains. Textured velvet wallpaper lined the walls, a set of Persian rugs covered the hardwood floor, and all other surfaces were swathed in either satins or silks, creating a soft space that was both inviting and intimate. The furnishing were sparse: a long dresser with a central cabinet and many drawers, a small circular table just big enough to seat four, and banks of pillows in various sizes. Martinez wondered if this was Keller's attempt at re-entering the womb.

She started with the dresser, which bore a few pieces of metalwork, a Tibetan singing bowl, and the remains of a smudge stick resting in an ashtray. Inside the drawers were the various accoutrements of magical practice: candles, matches, incense, chalk. Then there were things specific to Keller's practice: crystals, essential oils, various bottles of dried herbs and viscous fluids. Martinez was relieved she didn't find a mini-fridge up here—less of a chance Keller was making deals with devils, which usually required blood payment.

Martinez ran her gloved hand over the mahogany of the cabinet in the center of the dresser, tracing the scrollwork, fans, and flowers with her fingertips. The wear on the brass pulls told Martinez this compartment was frequently accessed. Within the repository was a crystal ball, perched on its polished wooden platform and covered with a black silk scarf. A small bronze hand mirror was secured in a velvet bag.

If her crystal ball is in here, what's on the table? Martinez wondered as her attention turned to the covered object lying in the center of the circular surface. She pulled back the sheet to reveal the table was little more than a slate slab supported by a metal framework. The faint traces of old chalk were still present, thoroughly wiped but not completely cleaned away. In the middle of the table lay a spherical mirror framed in a tessellated blue and white mosaic on teakwood. Plunged into the middle of the shattered mirror was a plain dagger.

The hairs on the back of her neck stood up. She cast her last two rounds of salt and saw two patterns: one was clearly Keller's, but the other was distinctly different. Martinez snapped a picture on her phone and weighed her options, rolling an oblong stone in her pocket. All its rough edges and grit had been worn over years of water erosion, and it was one of the last pieces of kit entrusted to her by Weber, the Salt Mine's armorer. The mature inventor was hardly the sort to coddle, but he'd given her a genuine lecture about the dangers of using the hag stone and how to use it responsibly.

She fished the smooth stone from her pocket and peered through the hole bored into its core. Martinez counted the seconds in her head as she hastily swept the room in true sight, and pulled the hag stone away from her eye before she got to ten—there wasn't a safe amount of time to look through a hag stone, but the shorter the better, lest the barrier between realms got too thin. The last thing she needed was fae. Or worse.

Martinez carefully wrapped the impaled mirror so none of the shards would be lost. The mirror itself wasn't magical, but the dagger piercing it glowed the most peculiar shade of amethyst through the stone.

Chapter Five

Detroit, Michigan, USA
5th of August, 1:30 p.m. (GMT-4)

Detective Cerova pulled up to The Lofts, the latest lifestyle apartments that had invaded Detroit's downtown. She presented her badge to the doorman, who quickly whisked her into the building and pointed her in the general direction of the elevators. She rode up to the tenth floor along with a polished woman in her mid-forties carrying a dog that was only marginally larger than her clutch purse.

The elevator panel had buttons for the gym, the pool, and the concierge—which Cerova had only associated with hotels up until now. The rents here were twice as much as her mortgage, and Cerova was pretty sure that was the proverbial lemon her elevator mate was sucking on given her persistent pucker. *That's the price of living the lifestyle…* Cerova mused as she brushed past her when the elevator doors opened.

A bevy of activity came in and out of the open door of Unit 1005. Cerova ducked under the crime scene tape and entered a world of tall ceilings, open floor plans, decorative kitchens with top-of-the-line appliances, and sleek modern design. Collins caught sight of his partner and beckoned her deeper into the apartment. "Some place, right?"

"The only way this place could be more magical is if Willy Wonka showed up on a river of chocolate," Cerova quipped.

He chuckled. "I'm pretty sure there's enough room to stash a hoard of Oompa Loompas in the walk-in closet." He flipped open his notepad and filled her in. "Deceased is Emily Schappel, age twenty-six. The body was discovered at 12:45 by her fiancé; she was supposed to meet him at noon for cake tastings and when she didn't show and he couldn't reach her by phone, he got worried and came over. She works for a real estate development company. We checked with her office and she didn't show up for work this morning—very unlike her, according to her supervisor. The last time her fiancé communicated with her was last night; apparently, they always say goodnight to each other over the phone."

He handed her a pair of gloves before they entered the expansive bathroom; Cerova was pretty sure she'd had bedrooms that were smaller than this. The sink and toilet lined one wall; the far wall housed an oversized tub with a rainfall showerhead. Opposite the sink was a built-in vanity with drawers, cabinets, and a plush seat sized to tuck under the countertop. The robed body of Emily Schappel was still seated with her torso bent over, resting on the counter. Her straight blonde hair fanned across the top of the vanity, partially covering the assortment of beauty products—all high-end and top-dollar. *Like gilding a lily*, Cerova lamented at the beautiful deceased young woman.

Doug Knoll greeted the detectives. "Fancy seeing you two here. We have to stop meeting like this—people will talk."

Cerova was usually up for his quirky humor, but not today. "What do you have for us, Doug?"

"According to liver temp and lividity, she died five to seven hours ago. Petechial hemorrhage and periorbital cyanosis without ligature marks or contusions…sound familiar?" he said suggestively.

"Even down to the fingerprints all over the mirror," Collins commented. "Are they hers?"

"That's for *your* techs to figure out, but that's where the smart money is," the ME replied.

"Any obvious connection between Janice Keller and Emily Schappel?" Cerova carefully examined the body and the contents on the counter; the deceased had been in the middle of making up her face, with one eye painted and the other bare.

"I've got uniforms making inquiries, but Keller isn't a listed contact in her phone and the fiancé doesn't recognize the name or face," Collins replied.

"You have a cause of death for Keller yet?" Cerova grilled Knoll.

"I was in the middle of the write up when I got the call to come here. Officially, it's asphyxia: mechanism unknown. Unofficially, it's weird as hell. Unless someone found a way to throw her into space for two minutes and put her back into the ladies' bathroom before the water in her body exploded on a cellular level and swelled her up like a Macy's Thanksgiving Day Parade balloon, I don't know how she died, just what killed her."

Cerova's eyes flickered back and forth between the magnified table mirror and the vanity mirror that multiplied her reflection with the mirror above the sink. "What is it?" Collins asked his partner, sensing a quandary.

"Why are there so many fingerprints on the big mirror and none on the small one?" Cerova posited the question. "The whole point of having a vanity is to *sit down* and get ready. Sure, you have to get up close to finish the eyes, but that's what this guy is for." She motioned to the freestanding table mirror.

"Maybe she stood up when she was losing oxygen and the fingerprints are her grasping on the way down," the ME took a stab.

"You're struggling for breath, but nothing gets knocked off the vanity? Even her facial creams and makeup are still in order," she observed. "Something is definitely off about this whole scene."

Knoll flagged some techs over. "Let me get the body back to the morgue and see what I can find. In the meantime, I think there's someone you guys should talk to. I had a visitor this morning asking about Janice Keller, a woman from the FBI."

Cerova and Collins gave each other a puzzled look. Once they nonverbally verified that neither of them had been contacted by the FBI, she finally spoke, "What do they want with Janice Keller?"

"Apparently, she was helping them with a case, but I didn't get much else out of her. Special Agent Martinez, that is," Knoll clarified. "Keller's even less talkative."

Chapter Six

Detroit, Michigan, USA
5th of August, 5:30 p.m. (GMT-4)

"Thanks for helping me out," Martinez called back as she approached the front door.

"No problem. Scrying and divination can be really tricky, especially when you are trying to use someone else's kit," Joan Liu, code name Aurora, responded. The slim Asian woman was dressed casually in jeans and a t-shirt with minimal makeup, and her short hair had the just-rolled-out-of-bed look that took a surprisingly long time to achieve intentionally. "Plus, you had me at 'home-cooked meal.'" She was only half joking—her fridge was pretty much condiments, spoiled dairy products, and take-out leftovers well past their prime.

Martinez laughed, but under the surface, she was frantically trying to remember the last time she'd actually cleaned the house and hoped she hadn't left any underwear conspicuously laying about. "Well, I hope you like pot roast," she spoke before unlocking the door. Liu was the first visitor she'd had since she moved to Detroit, and a last-minute one at that.

Martinez had tried not to take work home with her, but when she'd presented the information and items she'd gathered at Keller's to Chloe and Dot, they'd decided to divide and conquer. Doing divination within the Salt Mine was out of the question; due to the wards and being surrounded by salt, it was not possible to engaged in transplanar shenanigans, which meant scrying rituals had to be performed at a secure off-site location. Being conjoined twins, the librarians couldn't exactly split up with one staying to conduct research and the other performing magic at Martinez's. Martinez could have given it a shot, but admittedly, she wasn't great at scrying, even though she had managed to pass her agent testing, when Wilson took something from her house and she'd had to scry to find it. When they'd recommended Liu as the next best thing, it had been an easy sell. Liu was a lousy cook and voraciously inhaled any baked goods Martinez brought to work. For such a small person—she was 5'4" and maybe 130 pounds soaking wet— she could pack it away.

The mouthwatering smell of a slab of beef roasting in its own juices for hours in the slow cooker filled their nostrils. Liu's stomach growled in reply. "You can put your stuff down anywhere." Martinez motioned toward the living room on her way to the kitchen. "Can I get you anything to drink?"

Liu placed her bag down beside the couch and took everything in. It was homey and tasteful without being boring or kitschy, but it wouldn't win any design competitions. "I'd love a glass of wine, but perhaps I should stick to tea until after the magic is done," she hollered. "You need any help in there?

I can't cook worth shit, but I make a decent sous chef," she chuckled at her own private joke—there was none better with knives and blades than Aurora.

"You're more than welcome to cut some tomatoes, radishes, and cucumbers for the salad. I also have a nice crusty loaf of bread that needs slicing," Martinez spoke over the clatter of dishes, glasses, flatware, bowls, and lids.

Liu wandered into the kitchen and expertly grasped the chef's knife, appraising its balance and sharpness. "So this was Wilson's place?" she asked incredulously as she started working on the first tomato.

"That's who I send the rent to," Martinez replied as she grabbed the olive oil and balsamic vinegar and whisked together a dressing for the salad.

"It seems so…normal," Liu commented.

"Yeah, it's weird to think of Wilson doing normal things like laundry or mowing the lawn," she politely agreed.

"Or fixing a car in a wife beater," Liu added. The mental picture made Martinez burst into honest laughter. Liu approved. The whistle blew on the kettle, and Martinez offered her a mug and the tea caddie.

Liu didn't know much about Wilson; he kept to himself and they'd only had incidental interactions on missions. They had started at the Salt Mine around the same time, but he rebuffed any attempts at camaraderie early on and Liu never felt the need to ask twice. There were more agents back then—nearly a dozen—and if she needed a consult, she generally found a friendly ear somewhere else. She couldn't imagine what it was like to be trained by Wilson.

Liu steeped a bag of Earl Grey and returned to chopping. Martinez caught the whirling gleam of the blade as she made quick work of the fixings and tossed the salad in the dressing. Martinez excavated the pot roast from the crockpot onto a platter, spooning the potatoes, carrots, and pearl onions around it. Then she poured the juices into a gravy separator and grabbed the baguette. "So, what's the plan for tonight? Magically speaking?" she asked as she handed the loaf to Liu. "Chloe and Dot were light on the details, only that it couldn't be done within the Salt Mine." Martinez moved everything over to the table.

"Well, first we try to get information from her various divination tools," Liu responded, taking a seat. "Sort of like scrying the scryer. With any luck, we'll be able to see what Janice was up to in the days before her death."

"And if that doesn't work?" Martinez started on her salad while Liu went straight for the fork-tender roast.

"Then we say we tried and pop open a bottle of wine." Liu smiled. It was the only time any lines appeared on her porcelain face. It was hard to nail down her age; given the right accoutrement and social cues, Liu could present herself anywhere from late twenties to late forties. "So, how are you finding Detroit?"

Martinez was throw off balance by the question; it had been a while since she'd had a social meal that wasn't a pretense on a mission. "Summer is a lot nicer than winter, but I've got a few months before I have to find a good snow blower."

"Less time than you think," Liu cautioned her with the tip of her fork. "I remember the first time I was sent away for a mission during winter—to fricking Thailand! The locals were bundled up in 60°F weather, and I was doing a dance in my sarong that I wasn't knee deep in snow." Liu noticed Martinez freeze up. "What? Was it something I said?"

Martinez blinked and spontaneous facial movement resumed. "No, I'm just not used to talking about work with anyone, especially not someone who really understands what I do. For all the time I spent training with Wilson, I can honestly say we didn't do much talking about things outside of the missions."

Liu pushed food around her plate and tested the waters. "There are a lot of ways to be an agent of the Salt Mine. Being an island works for Wilson, but that is certainly not the only way." She looked up and regarded Martinez—it had seemed to find purchase. "I understand why he does it. He thinks it makes it safer for everyone…not just for him, but for anyone he should happen to care about. But in my experience, if you don't have somewhere, something, or someone to go and get perspective, you get sloppy and make mistakes."

They took a few bites in silence until Martinez spoke

evenly. "One of the first things he told me during my interview was how many agents had died in the past couple of years." Liu searched for a hint of emotional context, but couldn't find anything.

"Don't get me wrong, it's a dangerous job and getting dead is always an option, even when you do everything right," Liu qualified. "We knew that when we signed up, but accepting the possibility of death is not the same thing as figuring out how to live with this job. It can be a real mind fuck."

Martinez's face broke into a smirk—something about having Aurora swearing over her Earl Grey was infinitely comical to Martinez.

"What?" Liu puzzled.

"Just imaging Leader's face reading that on a hypothetical employee feedback card." Martinez relaxed and finished her salad, sopping up the last of the vinaigrette with her bread.

"Feh, she's got nothing on my grandmothers. You want impassive older women constantly judging you when you have no hope of measuring up? Go Asian," Liu joked with ease. "At least Leader will never badger me about when I'm getting married and having kids."

"Probably because she already knows the answer," Martinez snarked. "She knew my ring size, and I know that wasn't on any of the HR forms."

Liu chuckled, which elicited a giggle from Martinez. Liu took another bite of meat with potato. "This pot roast is delicious."

Martinez dished some on her plate. "Thanks. The trick is onion soup mix and a little red miso."

*****

With the dishes cleared, Liu grabbed her bag and set everything up on the dinner table. First, she placed a rubber mat to protect the wood and then pulled out a sixteen-by-sixteen slate tile from her bag. "Portable, cheap to replace when it cracks, and no kneeling required," she tipped off Martinez. Liu started chalking the circle and runes while Martinez arranged the tea lights at the key points. When Liu was finished, Martinez pulled out Keller's crystal ball and placed it in the center of the circle, making sure it remained covered until Liu was ready to start the ritual.

Martinez lit the candles and they joined hands. Ideally, there would have been at least three people to help power the magic, but they were banking that two actual practitioners should be more than enough. Liu pulled off the cover and started chanting while Martinez threaded her will through her hands and into Liu's. A gray fog filled the glass dome. Bolstered by Martinez, Liu dove into the mist, beckoning the guides to show her what had already been seen. She flattered them, beseeched them, and appealed to their sense of justice—one of their own had been cut down and perhaps a vision held the key.

The haze parted, revealing what Janice Keller had seen when last she peered into the ball. An hour-glassed dark-haired beauty emerged in a flowing silk robe. Martinez recognized the figure from Keller's drawings—the nude by the water. The woman in the crystal ball propped up her foot on a chair, her shapely leg in black stockings secured with a garter belt. She brushed her robe aside and unfastened a sheathed dagger from high on her thigh and placed it within a drawer in her vanity. Martinez couldn't be certain, but it could be the dagger she'd found at Keller's. The figure in the glass turned her head abruptly—perhaps a knock at the door? She shut the drawer quickly, fluffed up her hair, and arranged her robe so the top draped a little more. The image vanished in a puff of smoke swirling within the sphere. Liu praised the guides for their generosity and wisdom before covering the crystal ball and releasing Martinez's hands.

"I'd call that a result," Liu spoke definitively. "Apparently, the guides were quite fond of Janice. They actually wailed when I told them of her death, a rare expression of attachment for their kind."

"Can we do that with the mirrors?" Martinez inquired.

"The broken mirror? No. Maybe Chloe and Dot could, but not me. The bronze mirror…maybe I could steam it?" Liu spoke equivocally.

Martinez checked her tone before speaking. "What exactly do we need for that?" she neutrally asked.

Liu laughed. "You don't have to be careful with my feelings. I know how crazy I sound sometimes." She dampened a kitchen towel and wiped the slate tile clean. "Basically, I do a little magic, hold the mirror up to a source of steam, let it fog up, and see if something presents itself."

Martinez put the kettle back on the burner and narrowed her eyes. "You just want another cup of tea, don't you?"

"Are you kidding? I'm working my way toward wine," Liu exclaimed as she put away her supplies and pulled out her spell focus: three Chinese coins knotted to each other with red ribbon through their square centers. It briefly crossed Martinez's mind just how stereotypical magic was—*Liu uses feng shui coins to focus and I, a Latina, use a rosary*? She knew it wasn't racist, but it sort of felt like it.

The rooster-shaped stopper on the end of the kettle started crowing, and Liu pooled her will into a knot and shot it like a cannon toward the mirror as she held it above the steam. The vapor covered the polished surface and Liu pulled it back, watching the rivulets of water run down the bronze. A series of symbols escaped erasure, and Martinez snapped a picture. She taped out a quick message and sent it the Salt Mine, attention to Chloe and Dot, who were working on the magical signature at Keller's that wasn't in the database, the dagger—which Dot had informed her was a Finnish puukko of some age—and who or what could suck the breath out of a person.

Liu checked her phone while Martinez tapped away with

her thumbs. "I'm afraid I'm going to have to take a rain check on the wine—duty calls."

"Anything that would require my backup?" Martinez said before thinking. She was actually enjoying spending time with her.

Liu smiled enigmatically. "Babysitting a toddler is a little like banishing a demon, but I think I'll be okay on my own. Mind if I use your restroom before I hit the road?"

Martinez pointed her in the right direction before she wiped the condensation off the bronze hand mirror and returned it to its velvet bag. A niggling thought bubbled to the surface.

"Is it true that breaking a mirror is bad luck?" Martinez asked as Liu exited the restroom.

Liu shrugged as she hoisted her bag on her shoulder. "For a diviner who uses mirrors, it's a pretty big loss, but I don't know about bad luck."

Martinez's brow furrowed. "So what would make Janice break a mirror?"

"Maybe whatever she saw on the other side of the mirror was worse." Liu reached over and gave Martinez a half hug with her free arm. "Thanks for dinner. Call me if you need any more help…and you owe me wine." Martinez closed her front door and watched Liu's car pull out into the street.

She headed to the kitchen to deal with dishes and pack up leftovers, replaying the evening's conversation. It was enjoyable, but the suspicious part of her was looking for angles. Liu hadn't probed into her past or fished for any information about her missions, and neither of them made any reveals of importance. It was just two colleagues having dinner before knocking out an assignment. It was nice to have someone to chat with over dinner, and she hadn't laughed that much with another person in a while, but she'd really picked the wrong profession for making friends.

She secured Keller's three reflective surfaces she'd brought home and checked the time; she could always stop by the Mine before her last stop of the day. Once her vape pen saltcaster was refilled with superfine salt, Martinez went upstairs to get ready.

Chapter Seven

Intellectually, Detective Jennifer Cerova knew it wasn't a competition. By all accounts, the FBI had first rights to Janice Keller if she was working with them before her death. As long as the bad guy got caught, that was what's important. Sure, she had a hunch that Emily Schappel's and Janice Keller's deaths were somehow connected, but until she could find something to link them, there was little hope of interdepartmental cooperation. Which was why she was trawling the depths of social media instead of listening to her sister tell her about her day.

"…and that's when the giant tyrannosaurus rex gave birth to an ocelot in the parking lot," Mira concluded her story.

Jenny looked up from her laptop. "What?!"

"That's the part that got your attention? Not the elephants marching through my lobby?" Mira asked skeptically. "We're supposed to be having dinner together and you're surfing the net."

"I'm not blowing you off for cat videos. I'm working," Jenny defended herself and took a bite of her burger. "And you showing up at my place with take-out isn't the same as having dinner together."

"I remembered no pickles and onion rings instead of fries," Mira gave herself credit. "Is this about the woman we found at the club?"

"Sort of. I'm no longer on the case, but I could be if I found a connection to a body I found this afternoon," Jenny spoke in non-specifics.

Mira looked over her sister's shoulder and skimmed the thumbnails of photos featuring a pretty young blonde. "Is that her?"

"Yeah, but I can't find a connection between her and the woman we found at 18 is 9, and it's killing me because I know their deaths are somehow related." Jenny threw her hands up in frustration.

Mira knew that look, like a dog that wouldn't let go of a chew toy—the harder you tried to pull it out of its mouth, the tighter it chomped down. After washing down the most recent bite of her bacon cheeseburger with a sip of soda, the younger Cerova took the computer out of Jenny's lap and directed her to her food. "Eat before it gets cold. I've got this," she said confidently. "You may an expert in solving murders, but I cyberstalk like a pro."

Stunned by her younger sister's assertiveness, Jenny took direction; after the second bite, she realized just how hungry she was. After five minutes of scrolling, Mira piped up, "Got something."

"Shut up!" Jenny squished next to her on the couch. "Don't get too excited. I didn't find a picture of them as secret lovers, but your blonde was at 18 is 9 last night." Mira handed Jenny back her laptop and tapped her finger on a mirror selfie. "That's the mirror in the ladies' bathroom on the main dance floor."

Jenny examined the picture closely for details. "Are you sure?"

Mira grabbed her phone and pulled up a picture of herself in front of the same set piece. "Everyone takes a selfie at that mirror. It's like it amplifies your hotness."

Jenny mulled it over. It was something, at least until the ME completed the autopsy and confirmed a similar cause of death and MO…although she wasn't thrilled with his space theory. If someone was picking their victims from the club… "Hey Mira, do me a favor and stay away from 18 is 9, at least until I figure out what happened to these women."

To Jenny's amazement, Mira didn't argue; she simply nodded. Jenny thought back—this was the second night in a row that Mira showed up at her place on short notice. Jenny closed her laptop and gave her sister her undivided attention for the first time since she'd showed up with food. "Are you doing okay?"

Mira shrugged, which loosely translated as "No, but I'm not sure I want to talk about it." Jenny just waited; her sister was not one to hold back for long. Eventually the silence broke. "I'm just a little freaked out being alone at my place. I'm fine during the day and at work, but when I come home to an empty apartment…"

It dawned on Jenny that Janice Keller was her sister's first dead body, and it didn't help that she was found somewhere her sister clearly frequented. Jenny reached over to her sister. "You're more than welcome to stay at my place for a while, at least until one of us kills the other."

Mira let herself be comforted. "Thanks."

"You know, cyber stalking totally makes you a creeper," Jenny teased her.

"No, cyber stalking is just a tool. Being creepy makes someone a creeper," Mira objected.

"Wanna eat ice cream and brutally judge ridiculous profiles on my dating apps?" Jenny suggested. "If a cute one comes up, you can use your powers for good."

Mira hugged her sister tight. "You know me so well."

Chapter Eight

Detroit, Michigan, USA
5th of August, 10:30 p.m. (GMT-4)

Aloysius Hardwick wasn't in the mood for making the rounds tonight, but he didn't have the heart to close 18 is 9. For some people, it was the only place they felt safe to be themselves, and Janice would have wanted the music to play on. Although he didn't want to socialize, he didn't want to be alone either, and took a seat in the corner where he could watch those untouched by the grief that burdened him dance, flirt, and have a good time. It reminded him of happier days.

He wasn't sure if it was a karmic kick in the pants or a twist of fate to amuse some bored deity that a homicide detective found the body. He'd spent much of the day with lawyers in a pre-emptive defense; it never looked good to have a corpse turn up at your establishment, even if you were innocent. The fact that it was Keller made it personal, not just for Hardwick, but for the magic community that congregated at his club.

The same thoughts rose whenever a practitioner died. Did she get in over her head and her karmic debt finally caught up to her? Did she get involved with someone or something sketchy? Whenever magic was a possibility, death by natural causes quickly became the outlier. Hardwick was the closest thing she had to family, and he had already made arrangements for her cremation once they released her body.

He was mulling over memories when a feminine voice broke his reverie. "You look like someone who could use a drink." His visual scan started with her black patent leather stilettos and the view just got better on the way up. Dressed in all leather, her clothing was more biker chick but her makeup was all goth, with heavy liner and dark lipstick. Her hoops were pure Latina. She was at least twenty years younger than him, but old enough to be interesting. She held out two tumblers filled with amber liquid as an added enticement. "Mind if I join you?"

"What's in the glass?" he played hardball.

"Laphroaig, old enough to vote but still young enough to unironically ask what payphones were," she remarked. "I'll even let you choose yours first so you don't have to worry about if I slipped something into your drink."

He guffawed and motioned to the chair next to him. "Aloysius Hardwick," he introduced himself, selecting a glass.

"Teresa Martinez," she responded in kind and took a seat. She sipped her beverage, and the smoky Highland peat flooded her palate. "See, perfectly safe."

"First time here?" he asked, even though he already knew the answer. He would have remembered a leggy Latina with juicy thighs.

She nodded. "I'm new in town and a friend of mine recommended the place."

"Oh, what's her name?"

She leaned in, all smiles. "His name is Wilson."

Hardwick took a long drink to give him time to think. "How is he doing? It's been a long time since he's been by."

She flipped her hair. "Oh, you know him: a workaholic. But I can't blame him; his job is *so* important." The glint in her eyes spoke volumes. She could see the gears churning in his head and held her smile.

He finished his drink and toyed with the empty glass in his large hand. "You know, I think I have something that's old enough to remember disco upstairs. Care to join me?"

She grabbed her glass. "Lead the way."

Martinez hadn't anticipated just how tall Hardwick was; even in her heels, he was still a bit taller. The amber pendent Weber had given her bounced against her chest as she came to her feet and accepted his arm—the twins had warned her she was totally Aloysius's type and she had sided with caution against any charm attempts. He led her to his private elevator instead of forcing her to take the stairs in those heels. The muscle standing guard summoned the elevator and stepped aside for Mr. Hardwick and his guest. Martinez noted the stops on the panel and the fact that Hardwick had to insert a key before selecting the second floor.

"In all the years we've known each other, Wilson's

never bought me a drink, much less a Laphroaig," he made conversation on the ride up.

Martinez sipped her drink. "You know, that doesn't surprise me." The elevator dinged and the doors opened to a lounge with a fully stocked bar, a dark fireplace, high ceilings, and leather couches. The exposed beams and brickwork kept the space authentic in spite of the touches of luxury and comfort. Given Hardwick's purple suit, yellow shirt, and green tie, Martinez was expecting more color and animal print in his personal domain and was pleased to find rich burgundies, dark sables, and deep blues instead.

She sunk into an oversized armchair, still working on her first drink while Hardwick poured himself something from a decanter. He took a seat across from her on the couch. "What can I do for an esteemed member of the Salt Mine?"

"I'd like to ask you a few questions about Janice Keller and inspect the area where her body was found," Martinez replied directly. "I understand you two had a long history."

He smiled fondly. "She wandered into 18 is 9 one night—a confused kid who didn't understand what was happening to her. Her foster family was Pentecostal, and they did some atrocious things to her in an attempt to 'banish Satan from her.' I'm not sure which was worse, the physical trials or the psychological damage. When she found a chance to run, she ran fast and far. I offered her a safe place to sleep, shower, and get a decent meal of her own volition. You can't come off too nice to people who are use to being kicked; it makes them suspicious and scares them off," he explained.

"Eventually, she started working here and I discovered she was quite well-read—spent a lot of time in libraries reading all the things that were 'against God,' so I helped her get her GED and start taking classes at the community college, which eventually turned into a BA of Library Science."

"All out of the kindness of your heart…" she commented.

"It wasn't like that," he said sharply. "I'm hardly a saint, but I'm not a predator. A lot of kids who are magically inclined don't make it, and despite all the shit life threw at her, she'd survived." He calmed himself down. "I considered it a mitzvah of sorts."

Martinez eased off. "So how did her magical abilities develop? I understand she was pretty good at divination and scrying."

"She was blessed with second sight—seeing things that had happened, were going to happen, or were happening in the present but far away. She didn't know how to control it or channel it, and when puberty hit, it got even worse. It took her six months of floating in and out of here before she felt comfortable telling me about it and longer to believe that she wasn't crazy, just gifted. Once she had some security in her day-to-day life, she was able to tackle that aspect of herself, with the help of magicians that practiced within that same discipline."

"Sounds like Janice Keller's family was 18 is 9," she

observed.

"I think that's a fair statement," he concurred.

"Yet her lifeless body was found here."

Hardwick winced. "Yes, in the ladies' room in the basement."

"On the ground floor, I saw a bodyguard standing in front of the stairs down; it that a standard precaution or something recent?"

Hardwick shook his head. "Always in place. The basement is for private engagements and open-play events for our BDSM clients, so the need for privacy is paramount."

"And the third floor?" Martinez asked.

"Those are my private quarters," he answered with a mischievous gleam in his eyes.

"Does anyone else have access to the elevators except for yourself?" Martinez let the insinuation slide.

"No, and the bouncer didn't see anyone else go downstairs after Janice. There were only three people down there at the same time, and they were engaged in the dungeon the whole time," he filled in the gaps. "I take it Janice didn't die naturally, if you are looking into her death."

"There are irregularities that warrant investigation," Martinez responded vaguely. "Do you know of anyone who would want to harm her—anyone she had recently fought with, any trouble she might have been in?"

"I'm not one to pry," he prefaced in a tone that told

Martinez he was *totally* the sort to pry, "but I think Janice and Scarlet had a spat recently."

"Scarlet?"

"Mistress Scarlet, the pro-dom that runs the basement playroom," he elaborated.

"Professional or private disagreement?"

"You would have to ask Scarlet," he retreated tactfully.

Martinez went out of a limb. "Does 'the Hollow' mean anything to you?"

Hardwick's brow furrowed. "No, I can't say that it does. Should it?"

"It was one of the last things on Janice's mind," Martinez downplayed its importance before finishing her drink. "I guess my next stop is the basement." The sound of leather on leather squeaked as she rose from the armchair. "Give me a ride down?"

As he finished his second drink, Hardwick decided he definitively preferred her company to Wilson's and mimed "ladies first" into the elevator.

They rode down in silence, both sizing up the other without overtly gawking. As the elevator doors opened to the basement, Hardwick stepped out and directed Martinez down the hall. He paused outside the door of the ladies' restroom. "I'm assuming you'll want some privacy to do your thing," he commented vaguely for the benefit of anyone listening.

Martinez gave him an appreciative nod and headed inside. The place had been cleaned and any evidence of the body or the police was gone, but that was of little concern to Martinez—what she was looking for wouldn't fade unless it was erased. She pulled out her vape pen, lined up the notches, and salted the room. She stood in the center, waiting for patterns to emerge, and got distracted by how great her ass looked in the mirror. *The burpees are working*, she thought as she appraised herself in the full-length mirrors from various angles.

In time, four distinct patterns emerged: three she recognized and one new to her. The first was Keller's. The second was Hardwick's, which she'd pulled before she left the Salt Mine. The third was the same unknown signature that was in Keller's house. She pulled out her phone and snapped photos. Martinez scrolled through her gallery to make sure the pictures were good when she noticed that the picture of the fourth signature was different than what she saw with her own eyes.

She cleared her mind and focused her will on the fourth pattern. *Hail Mary, full of grace…* The salt shimmered and came back into focus, and the magical signature now matched the photo on her phone. *Curiouser and curiouser*, she said to herself as she released her will and drew a rough sketch of the magical signature as she originally saw it. With a swift kick, she disrupted the salt and dispersed the magic—salt casting for signatures as a method of creature and caster identification was a Salt Mine trade secret.

Hardwick was still waiting outside when she remerged. "Everything satisfactory?"

"Just one question, Mr. Hardwick: what did you do to the mirrors in there?" Martinez quizzed him.

He grinned. "Just a little glamour—everyone likes to look their best when they're going out. And please, call me Aloysius."

Chapter Nine

Detroit, Michigan, USA
6th of August, 2:00 a.m. (GMT-4)

Michael gently placed his keys on the side table and kicked off his shoes, careful not to wake the rest of the house. It had been a slow night at work, and the only reason he'd picked up the shift from one of the other bouncers was that Mira was supposed to be working tonight. By the time he found out she had called off—something about a family emergency—he was solidly on the hook.

He changed out of his black muscle shirt and jeans and into his workout clothes. It had been nearly a week since he'd put up his last video, and he was a firm believer in consistency. His online weightlifting channel already had a little over a hundred thousand followers, and it wouldn't grow if he didn't stick with it.

He headed down to the partially finished basement and flipped on the light. It had been an investment to put in a home gym, but he never had to wait for a bench to open up or hunt down the right weight. He'd started filming his lifts for personal improvement, but after a little encouragement from one of his roommates, he'd started posting them and making videos about how to lift with good form and avoid injury. For all his years of experience powerlifting, it felt good to share something he felt passionate about. Currently, he was working on different ways to isolate and work specific muscle groups for lifters who had maxed out on the more routine lifts. It was equal parts science and creativity, and Michael always liked a challenge.

He warmed up, watching himself in the full-sized mirror he had installed along one wall. He wasn't the biggest or the strongest dude, but he was nothing to sneeze at, and unlike the curlbros at the gym, he never skipped leg day. As his ex-girlfriend once noted, the saying might be "curls for girls," but it wasn't biceps pushing hips in bed.

As he bent down to rack the weights on the bar, he caught movement out of the corner of his eye. He turned his head toward the mirror and locked eyes with his reflection. Michael stopped what he was doing, drawn to his mirror image—on the sheen of sweat that was just starting to form on his skin and the cut of his muscles. He saw new depths in his deep brown eyes and stepped forward to get a closer look, until he was almost touching the glass.

He couldn't figure out why he was smiling, but he must have been if his reflection was. His fingertips reached out to the mirror and touched the image of his face, grinning ear to ear even as he felt himself become lightheaded. There were spots of light in his vision as he dropped to his knees, pressing his hands against the glass to reach beyond but failing. His eyelids grew heavy and his head emptied as he fainted, tumbling sideways onto the floor.

The grin of Michael's reflection morphed into a sinister sneer as it inhaled the last of his breath. Fed but not sated, his chiral form sunk deeper into its side of the mirror until all that remained was the two-dimensional reflection of Michael's collapsed body.

Chapter Ten

Detroit, Michigan, USA
6th of August, 8:15 a.m. (GMT-4)

Martinez picked through the boxes of evidence regarding the death of Janice Keller in her office at the FBI's Detroit Headquarters. Technically, she wasn't assigned an office and her name wasn't on any registries, but if anyone was checking internally, Teresa Martinez had transferred to the Detroit branch earlier this year with a promotion to special agent. There was no way for someone to contact Special Agent Martinez unless she gave them the information. The phone number went directly to the Salt Mine, answering as the FBI, taking messages with reassurances that Special Agent Martinez would return their call at her earlier convenience.

On the occasions that a physical location was required, the Salt Mine had secured an office in the building that could be used with the change of a nameplate. They even moved the furniture around and added personal touches so it looked like a different office, in case an individual had cause to repeatedly meet different Salt Mine agents in their FBI aliases. Martinez had put her request in for the office yesterday when she petitioned to move Janice Keller's death under FBI investigation. Not only did she need somewhere for the Detroit PD to deliver all the case materials, Martinez had a feeling she wasn't done with Detroit PD's finest. Detective Cerova had already left her three messages in twelve hours, and the last had been the most intriguing—a second victim with similar presentation as Keller, who visited 18 is 9 the night before her untimely death.

Martinez had stopped by The Lofts as soon as she got the message, unfortunately on her way home from 18 is 9. Her badge had been more than enough to get her into Unit 1005, despite the night concierge's reluctance at her attire. Unlike the bathroom at the club, The Lofts hadn't cleaned up the scene and Martinez had free reign. When she'd salted the area, the same unknown signature from Keller's home and the basement ladies' bathroom had emerged in the white grains. Martinez had pinned down the murderer's signature, except she didn't know who or what it belonged to. It confirmed, however, that Janice Keller's death was no longer an isolated incident.

The Detroit Field Office was in the heart of downtown and just down the street from her house in Corktown, which allowed her thirty minutes of extra sleep after her long day and late night. She searched through boxes of photos, physical evidence, witness statements, and case notes, looking for any hint of what Keller might have been up to magically. The photos of the mirror resembled the crime scene at The Lofts: covered in the victim's fingerprints. Whatever killed Keller at 18 is 9 had visited her house first, most likely through the mirror. Was that why there was a dagger stabbed into it?

Martinez opened a new box and carefully went over Keller's personal possessions at time of death. Besides a bit of chalk on her sleeve—presumably from her slate table—and a blue and white charm warding off the evil eye, there wasn't anything enlightening or incriminating on the magic front.

Martinez took advantage of the FBI's databases and pulled up Leigh Meyer, aka Mistress Scarlet. When she pulled up Meyer's photo ID, Martinez clicked her tongue in affirmation: Janice Keller had been spying on Meyer in her crystal ball. Meyer had told Detroit PD that their relationship was not personal, but perhaps she would have a different story for the FBI. After getting a home address and checking Meyer's record—nothing more than a few parking tickets—Martinez moved on to Jennifer Cerova.

Originally from Ann Arbor, Michigan, she held a Bachelors of Arts in Criminal Justice Studies from University of Michigan. After graduation, she'd joined the Detroit police department, within four years made detective, and worked her way to homicide three years ago. Her case closure rate was decent, and she didn't have any marks on her record. Martinez pulled up a photo; the thirty-one-year-old detective's oval face appeared on her screen. She looked like she was plucked out of the flashback scenes from *Godfather II*: an olive complexion with wavy brown hair, full eyebrows, an aquiline nose, and inscrutable deep-set brown eyes. Martinez pulled her personal information: Cerova owned a home in Detroit, no listed marriages or children, parents still alive and living in Ann Arbor, one sister.

Martinez checked the time and started shutting everything down. She had a 10:00 a.m. appointment with Chloe and Dot, which she took as a good sign. It meant they had news; if they'd had nothing, they would have just sent a message. She'd gotten the broad strokes from her own research yesterday afternoon. Of all the horrid ways supernatural creatures could kill someone, not many creatures sucked the breath out of their victims.

There were fae that sucked the breath out of babies and young sleeping children, sometimes doing such in animal form, but they couldn't prey on adults that could defend themselves. The loss in power that fae experienced when they ventured too far from their homeland made sucking the breath out of a fighting adult target improbable. It was possible that one of the stronger fae could hunt in such a manner, but highly unlikely—they wouldn't debase themselves by being so intimate with mortals, which they universally considered quite ugly and unrefined.

There were air elementals, which could theoretically create pressure systems that could mimic vacuum conditions in a localized area, but elementals were passé and rarely used among modern practitioners. As platonic ideals of basic natural forces, they weren't the brightest, they were easy to defend against, and they naturally dissipated over time in the mortal realm, so keeping one around required constant energy. You might summon one to fill the pool after winter or blow the leaves off the lawn in fall, but that's about it.

Then there were the fiends, who generally preferred more violent methods, but there were those that feasted on souls—and in many languages the concept of soul and breath were so closely tied that it was hardly worth the semantic argument when you were standing over a corpse. Martinez didn't pick up any trace of aethermorphic feedback on Keller's body, but there wouldn't be any if she was experienced in dealing with devils or demons. There also weren't any fiendish traces at either crime scenes, but she didn't know if demons and devils could cover their magical tracks the same way magicians could, which was something she needed to find out. Of course, she couldn't discount the possibility of a magician summoning one of these creatures or casting a spell to similar effect, but to kill and scrub their signature twice in two days was knocking up the karmic debt to life-threatening levels unless you could drop a cool million in philanthropy to balance your karmic scales.

Martinez packed up a few things to take to the Mine, just in case there was something she was missing. She closed the blinds and left for her windowless office buried deep into the earth.

*****

"I brought donuts...tell me you have news!" Martinez bellowed as she walked past the stacks and to the librarians' desk. Dot poked her nose over her reading at the mention of donuts. Chloe smiled as Martinez placed the box on the counter and added, "And not just any donuts. Jelly-filled donuts!" That was enough to get Dot to put her book down and open the container; she quickly settled on a raspberry-filled.

"You didn't have to do that," Chloe cooed sweetly, grabbing a matching donut out from under her sister, which elicited an annoyed grunt out of Dot.

Martinez grinned. "Don't worry, Dot. I bought four of those—two each. I figured you guys were burning the midnight oil and could use a pick-me-up." A moment of silence passed as the powdered sugar went everywhere despite their best efforts.

"Which do you want first: the unknown signature or the dagger?" Chloe asked once a few bites were downed and a semblance of order was restored.

"Let's go with the signature. There's been another murder, and I found the same pattern at that crime scene as well as where Janice was killed," Martinez replied.

Chloe's frowned at the news of escalation. "The bad news is that we don't know who or what it belongs to, but we know it's old."

"Like really old," Dot emphasized. "It's the magical equivalent of the most basic of signatures. You know how early telephone numbers were only two or three digits? Well, if this was a telephone number, it would be a single digit."

"But it makes sense with what you sent us last night from the bronze mirror. It was Sumerian, loosely translated as 'the Hollow'," Chloe pointed out.

"As in 'the Hollow has arrived'?" Martinez called back to Keller's tip.

"Yes, but that's really an incomplete translation. It's more like a rapacious eternal void with insatiable hunger," Chloe grasped for more words to capture the true meaning.

"Lovely," Martinez remarked. "So how did Janice Keller and the Sumerian cookie monster come to cross paths?"

Chloe and Dot shared a look before Chloe answered, "We have a working theory."

"I'm all ears."

"Well, the word for the Hollow is just a few dots and dashes off of the logogram for the fertility goddess in Sumerian," Chloe speculated.

"So you're suggesting that Janice may have summoned an ancient creature that sucks the breath out of people due to a spelling error?" Martinez clarified their hypothesis.

"Oh no!" Chloe exclaimed. "If she had summoned it, we would all be dead. It's more likely that she drew its attention in an attempt to petition the Sumerian goddess."

"And it's more likely that it devours souls," Dot corrected the agent.

"Like we always say, grammar counts," Chloe added.

Martinez wasn't going to argue—she'd seen the disastrous results of sloppy work. "So how do we kill it?"

The twins stared blankly at her. "We don't know."

Martinez was dumbfounded by their admission. "What do you mean you don't know? You guys know everything."

"Sumerian is one of the oldest languages, and the few lines we found referencing the Hollow talked about how it ate itself into a torpor and how one should 'walk softly when the lion sleeps'," Chloe responded contritely. "We've petitioned Leader for additional resources but haven't heard back yet."

Martinez brooded quietly. She knew what was responsible for the deaths and that it was using mirrors somehow, but didn't know how to stop it. "What about the dagger?"

"Ah." Chloe pulled it from a drawer. "It's not magic but it is special. It's extraplanar."

"You're going to have to use more words," Martinez prompted them.

"We are here in the mortal realm, but there are other planes of existence: hell, the land of the dead, the land of the fae, the Magh Meall, etc. This dagger is made of the stuff of some other place besides the mortal realm. We aren't sure where, but we gave Weber a small sample to run some tests," Chloe explained.

"Which doesn't explain how Janice got her hands on it," Dot grumbled.

"I think I can shed some light on that," Martinez spoke up. "Aurora helped me see the last image Janice saw in her crystal ball, and it was the pro-dom from 18 is 9 putting away a sheathed dagger. My gut tells me that dagger is hers and Janice either borrowed it or took it, but I haven't had a chance to talk to Mistress Scarlet yet. She wasn't at the club last night."

Both Chloe's and Dot's faces lost color. "Oh, that's not good," Dot said bluntly.

"It would explain a lot," Chloe addressed her sister.

"The icy reception they gave each other at Stephen's party last week," Dot chimed in.

"The wards at Janice's house," Chloe added thoughtfully.

"And depending on what the blade is made of…" Dot hinted suggestively.

"Either of you two mind filling me in?" Martinez chirped up.

They exchanged glances and agreed that Chloe should break the news. "Mistress Scarlet's real name is Meridiana, and *technically* she's a succubus." Martinez had no words and repeatedly opened her mouth only to close it again when no question came out. "She's not a soul-sucking succubus anymore," Chloe qualified. "She's cursed to not be evil."

"And banished from hell," Dot added.

"But she makes the best of it," Chloe concluded.

"Well, it's good to know she's a glass-half-full kind of devil," Martinez quipped. She quickly recalled everything she'd read about succubi and incubi—different names for the same type of devil, depending on if they took a female or male form.

Bred among devils to spy on each other, succubi were masters of seduction and disguise, with the ability to take any form and become that being. "So that duel signature I found at 18 is 9 last night?"

"The one in the photo is hers and the one you saw is Leigh Meyer, the form she's currently taking. We didn't think anything about it because Meridiana uses that bathroom all the time and she literally couldn't kill Janice," Chloe replied.

"And you let me go into 18 is 9 without telling me there was a succubus working there?!"

"It's not supposed to be common knowledge. If you had tried to look up her signature in the system, you wouldn't have gotten anything and the search would have been flagged higher up," Chloe explained.

"And you had nothing to worry about," Dot backed up her sister while simultaneously dismissing Martinez's concerns. "You promised to wear Weber's periapt to the club, and there wasn't a chance of her taking on your form. Don't you remember the unity of being ritual we did on you when you first accepted the job?" Martinez struggled to remember all the various hoops she had to jump through during onboarding; at the time, she hadn't read much about magic or the supernatural.

Martinez's anger was cut short with an epiphany, "Wait, if it's not common knowledge, how did Janice Keller know?"

The twins looked puzzled. "I guess that's something else you're going to have to ask Meridiana." Chloe pushed the plain-looking dagger forward. "Bring this. It should help ease the introduction."

Chapter Eleven

Detroit, Michigan, USA
6th of August, 11:00 a.m. (GMT-4)

Harold Weber put down his tools and flipped up the magnifying lens over his glasses at the sound of the electric kettle. It was time for a cup of tea, one of the events that gave his subterranean days structure. He filled the pot with hot water and watched the leaves unfurl through the steam before closing the lid.

He was almost done with repairing the shattered mirror, just a few more mends and the glass would be restored. Only then did any of the Salt Mine practitioners have a chance of uncovering its role in Janice Keller's last days. It was tedious work but Weber liked a good challenge. First, he'd cleaned the oily substance coating the shards by placing them in a sonic bath; it was the gentlest way to remove the grime. His best guess was burned mugwort, probably from a smudge stick. It was a popular plant used in divination magic as it was thought to protect travelers and thresholds, and mirrors had long been regarded as gateways among magicians.

Once cleaned and dried, he'd carefully reassembled the fragments inside the frame, like a jigsaw puzzle with no picture and all the pieces were sharp, pointy, or both. Once he'd confirmed there were no missing pieces, he'd begun mending each joint, using just enough of his will to make it whole. It was very much a sympathetic restoration; the twins would be none too pleased if he overwhelmed whatever residual magic was there with his own.

Of course, the broken mirror was only half the quandary; there was the matter of the dagger that was found lodged into it. It was extraplanar, that much was plain from Lancer's description of it through the hag stone. While such items could be enchanted, this one was not. It was old and bore the name of the Finnish witch Louhi. When he had first examined it, he'd briefly entertained the notion that he was holding Sampo but dismissed such silliness—surely if Sampo existed, it would have been magic. Of course, some extraplanar material had inherent properties that seemed extraordinary in and of itself to humans in the mortal realm.

His initial inspection of the dagger ruled out origins from hell, the land of the fae, the Magh Meall, and the land of the dead, but there were a slew of other options to consider. He had hoped to have more time with it, but had to settle for a few shavings for later additional testing. If they couldn't get answers from the mirror, perhaps the nature of the dagger could shed some light on the situation.

Weber removed his work apron over his unruly gray hair and hung it on a hook anchored to the wall. He turned on some music and freed his mind from the precise concentration required for his work. Although he was as inquisitive as ever, he wasn't a young man anymore and relished these breaks. He poured his oolong through a strainer, satisfied with his first sip. He always felt a good cup of tea needed nothing but a calm mind, although he was not opposed to sugar in chai that was steeped in heated milk. When in Rome…. He was fondly recalling the time he was stuck on a hill in Mumbai during the monsoon with the most charming family when the end of the second movement of Mahler Symphony No. 1 ended. Teatime was over.

He donned his apron, securing the ties around his waist. This next bit was going to be tricky, and an ounce of prevention was worth a pound of cure. He moved his work to a separate inert clean room where there were no other magical items present and fished a piece of blue tailor's chalk from one of the apron's many pockets. The tip of his tongue stuck out of the right corner of this mouth as he drew the protective circle. While Weber had faith in the Salt Mine's security measures, he knew if there were any danger, it would come once the mirror was made whole. Weber couldn't be sure what, if anything, would happen should there be any lingering magic.

He double-checked his work before placing the mirror inside the circle and delicately fused the last two joints with his will; the glass glimmered as a whole piece once more. Weber held his breath as he peered at his handiwork: something unseen rippled below the reflective surface.

Weber quieted his mind and started singing in his head—
Freude, schöner Götterfunken, Tochter aus Elysium. He drew
deep from his well of power and imbued himself with true
sight. When he gazed back at the mirror, it no longer gleamed
in the light. The abysmal blackness swirled and a flash of white
blinked from the other side: a triple-irised eye that encompassed
the whole of the mirror. It pressed against the other side of the
glass but found no entry, and swam away for more promising
prospects.

Weber breathed a sigh of relief and dismissed his spell. The
astral projection disappeared and the glass shined once more.
Without disrupting the circle, he carefully laid a piece of fabric
over the reflective surface. Even though the wards of the Salt
Mine made any infiltration through the mirror impossible, he
heeded the words of his former countryman: if you stare into
the abyss, the abyss will gaze back into you.

Chapter Twelve

Detroit, Michigan, USA
6th of August, 12:00 p.m. (GMT-4)

Meridiana lifted the satin eye mask and peeked at the clock. Her room was cool and dark despite it being noon, but there was nothing to keep out the persistent banging on the door. She rolled to the edge of the bed and cursed her luck; she had been out all evening and had crawled into bed a little before five this morning. It had been fun while it lasted, but she could have used a few more hours of sleep. Succubi didn't need their beauty sleep, but they appreciated it.

"I'm coming," she shouted as she came down the stairs while securing her robe. Whoever it was would no doubt have been offended if she answered her own door naked, even though *they* were the one so rudely interrupting her rest. The knocking ceased, a tacit sign that she had been heard and they were willing to wait a little longer.

The bright sunlight spilled into the entryway as she pulled the door open, backlighting the tall Latina woman dressed in a navy pinstriped suit. "My name is Special Agent Martinez of the FBI. I'm here to speak to Leigh Meyer."

"I'm Leigh Meyer," the curvaceous resident answered, her

slightly tousled long black hair tumbled over her shoulders. "What exactly is this about?"

"I have a few questions to ask you about Janice Keller," Martinez replied.

She certainly has the look of a G-man, Meridiana thought. "I don't understand. I already spoke to the police this weekend. What does the FBI have to do with this?" Meridiana objected.

Martinez met her gaze. "The case has recently been reassigned to the federal level and some new evidence has come forward. We were hoping you could shed some light on the situation."

"Could I see some ID?" Meridiana requested before opening the door any farther.

"Certainly," Martinez complied. The two women appraised each other as they played out their respective roles.

Meridiana stepped aside and opened the door wide. "Please, come in."

Martinez said a Hail Mary in her head as she crossed the threshold, not to power any magic but for good luck. She had never accepted a devil's invitation before.

"I worked late last night and just woke up. Could we do this in the kitchen while I make some coffee?"

"Sure, no problem," Martinez replied, following her into the airy kitchen decorated in yellows and blues. "I was actually at 18 is 9 last night. I must have just missed you."

Meridiana was surprised to hear a commendable absence

of judgment in her statement. "No, I was working a private engagement off-site. Mistress Scarlet doesn't typically make house calls, but I make an exception for the famous, wealthy, and well-connected that want to unwind discreetly." She tossed a glance over her shoulder, "You want a cup?"

"I'm fine, thank you," Martinez politely declined.

"Suit yourself," she responded as she fiddled with her espresso machine. "I pull a great shot." She motioned for Martinez to take a seat at the counter. "So, what's this new evidence you want to talk to me about."

Martinez pulled the wrapped dagger from her pocket. "I believe I have something of yours, Meridiana."

The robed vixen continued steaming her milk without skipping a beat. "You aren't FBI, are you?"

"I'm a special branch," Martinez answered truthfully, pooling her will in case she needed to defend herself.

Meridiana added the frothy foam atop her cappuccino and took her first blissful sip. She turned to face Martinez and smiled. "You get credit for not trying shoot me with one of your banishment bullets like the last Salt Mine agent that crossed my path—ruined my favorite leather jacket."

"What happened? I thought you were banished from hell."

"Hell stamped 'return to sender' on *me*, but alas, the jacket wasn't salvageable." She leaned back and took another sip. "But that was ages ago, well before your time. Go on, tell me what you've brought." She waved a hand at the counter.

Martinez flipped back one corner of the cloth and showed her the blade. "We found this at Janice Keller's and uncovered evidence that suggests it was yours."

"I knew it!" the devil exclaimed with vindication. "She swore up and down she didn't take it, but I knew it. Why else would she suddenly have new wards barring my entrance into her house?"

Martinez shrugged and ambiguously remarked, "Bitches be crazy?" Meridiana's lyrical laugh filled the sunny kitchen. "I know what you told the police, but it doesn't sound like your intimate encounters were purely professional."

The devil shifted her shoulders. "We drifted in and out of each other's bedrooms. Janice was fun and full of life. When you have lived as long as I have, you learn to take what you can get when it comes."

"But you had a recent falling out?" Martinez prompted.

Meridiana sighed and took a seat; clearly, there was a story there. "Janice was a seeker of knowledge, and everywhere she looked, she saw the snow job of the patriarchy. Her particular focus was on religion, and she was on a quest to find the goddess, with a capital G. She was convinced that there was a singular force of creation, and that all the female deities represented throughout all the world's religions were merely avatars or aspects of this divine power. She figured the further back she went, the closer she would get to the truth." She paused to drink more caffeine—it was far too early for confessions without it.

"So she starts getting into Sumerian hard core, and I told her it was a bad idea. Modern practitioners often have this idealized notion of creatures that come to be regarded as deities; they think they are benevolent and care about mortals. I tried to tell her that even if she were to find the Goddess, she was more likely to crush her like an ant than bestow her blessings—early humans made sacrifices to protect themselves *from* their gods. By this point, her quest for the Goddess was borderline obsessive, and she wouldn't hear any of it. I mean, what do I know, I've only lived for millennia? She accused me of being unsupportive, dismissive, and held the fact that I could take a male form against me as I could reap the benefits of the patriarchy at any time. So we parted ways.

"Fast forward to a little over a week ago, when I discovered my dagger was missing. Naturally, I tried to scry it but it was being blocked. I immediately became suspicious and confronted Janice about it. She denied everything, but wouldn't let me into her house to check."

Martinez let the silence settle its narrator before speaking. "Does 'the Hollow' mean anything to you?"

Meridiana shook her head. "Is that what you think killed her?"

"Possibly, and whatever killed Janice took another life yesterday. If the few lines of Sumerian are to be believed, we are just seeing the beginning of the deaths. Any chance you happened to be anywhere around Mesopotamia when this thing was active and know how to shut it down?" Martinez threw it out there.

Meridiana smirked. "I like you. It's rare to find a G-man with a sense of humor. Apologies…G-woman. That was before my exile and a girl can't be everywhere at once, but I may be able to ask around."

"Out of curiosity, how did Janice know you were a succubus?"

Meridiana pushed up the sleeves of her robe with a fond smile. "She had her suspicions that I wasn't what I appeared to be and started poking around with her crystal ball. I told her in a fit of pillow talk—I may not be evil, but you can't say the same about the kind of beings you would have to ask to find out more about me," she said diplomatically.

"Who else knows?" Martinez probed.

"Close friends, your boss, and anyone else long-lived like myself," she answered vaguely.

"Does Aloysius know?" Martinez couldn't contain her curiosity.

"Ali?!" She guffawed. "No. He's sweet, but the worst gossip."

Martinez's brow furrowed. "How do you know Janice didn't tell him?"

"Because I enchanted her silence." She picked up her cup and finished her cappuccino. "What, it's not evil. It's a necessary precaution when you have a gregarious lover that thinks nothing of oversharing."

"Well, you're Leigh Meyer to me," Martinez reassured her, and the succubus nodded accordingly. "While you two were seeing each other, did Janice routinely cover her bathroom mirrors?"

She shook her head. "But it's been almost a month since I was last there. Normally, diviners cover their focuses when not in use, but a normal mirror? Seems a little paranoid. How else are you going to get ready in the morning?" Meridiana replied.

"Maybe not paranoid enough, considering she's dead," Martinez commented before changing subjects. "I've been given the green light to return your property to you. Can you give me some detail about it that only the rightful owner would know?"

Meridiana took her cup to the sink. "There are runes carved into the handle, the name I was using at the time: Louhi."

Martinez unwrapped the dagger and left it on the counter with her FBI card beside it. "If you find anything out, please give me a call. It's my job to make sure history doesn't repeat itself."

"Tells you a lot about mortals, doesn't it? All that writing for accounting and commerce, and they only carve out a few lines about their monsters."

Meridiana escorted the agent out of her home before returning to the dagger, caressing its handle and the line of its ever-sharp blade. It had been with her for a long time by human standards, gifted during a time when legends lived the epic stories. It was given to her by an old friend that understood the precarious and capricious whim of morality among mortals. She wasn't allowed to do evil, but defending herself from aggression was hardly evil, and under the right circumstances, neither was revenge.

Chapter Thirteen

Detective Marshall Collins was typing at his desk when Cerova returned from lunch with a skip in her step. Mira had just texted her that Derrick's new girlfriend had dumped him hard and publically. Jenny had severed all ties to him when they broke up and she knew she shouldn't engage, but couldn't resist the overwhelming wave of schadenfreude that rushed over her. "You're in a good mood," Collins commented suspiciously.

"Got some good news over lunch," she replied as she put away her things and settled in.

"So haven't checked your e-mail?" he probed cautiously.

"Lunch is my time. Unless it's a dead body, it can wait thirty minutes," she sassed. "Why do you ask?"

"Don't shoot the messenger," Collins prefaced, "but the FBI are interested in the Schappel case."

"What?!" Cerova angrily typed in her password and waited for her computer to wake up.

"Apparently, they caught wind that it might be connected to Janice Keller," he answered. "And it sounds like they are expecting more deaths. Chief told me if any other bodies come our way with a similar MO or cause of death, we're to notify Special Agent Martinez and give them access to the crime scene and evidence." Cerova was reading the e-mail as he spoke, parsing the diplomatic phrasing for "play nice," but she didn't catch a whiff of formal complaint against her in particular.

She pulled her hand across her hair, a tic her partner recognized as frustrated surrender. "This is all my fault. I called the number Doug gave us, trying to get back on the Keller case. I may have intimated that Schappel and Keller both had a connection to 18 is 9, hoping it would convince them to work interdepartmentally. Instead, we may lose two cases instead of just one."

To his credit, he did not deliver an incredulous stare or comment on her well-intentioned but naive unilateral move. Instead, he shrugged it off. "Don't beat yourself up. There will be other murders for us to solve," he sardonically replied. He was going to say more, but his phone rang. Cerova parsed his grunts and started grabbing her gear before he had even hung up the phone. "See? We have a body in a basement."

"Like manna from heaven," Cerova sarcastically remarked, jingling her keys in her hand, her way of asking who was driving.

Collins stood up and put on his blazer. "I won't even bitch about you driving."

Cerova smirked. "Sweet talker."

It wasn't that Collins was a bad driver; Cerova just regarded herself a better one. It was a fundamental truism to which she ascribed: people who drove stick paid more attention to the road, especially in bad traffic. Constantly having to up- and downshift made people more engaged in the act of driving, and they simply didn't have enough hands to text while driving.

The ME and uniforms were already on scene when they pulled up to the two-story house on the west side of town, almost but not quite in Dearborn. The neighbors that were home were watching the yellow tape and flashing lights, no doubt waiting for a glimpse of a body. Collins held the tape up for Cerova, who nodded back in thanks. They had worked together for almost three years, grinding down each other's rough spots into a functioning partnership. She no longer objected to small chivalric acts, and he made a conscious effort not to discount her capability despite her age.

Cerova flagged down an officer to get them up to speed. "Victim is Michael Gerrold, age twenty-four. Found by his roommates shortly after noon. They thought he was sleeping in after a late night at work—bouncer at a club—but when they found his room empty, they checked the basement where he'd set up a gym. No sign of forced entry and they don't think anything is missing. Victim's wallet and phone are still in his room. I was just about to check with the neighbors to see if they heard or saw anything last night."

"Thanks, Peter," she dismissed him as she crouched down to avoid the low ceiling of the basement stairs. "Doug, what have you got for us?"

The ME nodded at the detectives. "Time of death somewhere between one and three this morning. No marks or signs of struggle on the body, but honestly, the guy's ripped, so someone would have to be suicidal or stupid to attack him one-on-one. Normally, I would chalk this sort of scene as a sudden cardiac arrest, possibly aided by drugs, supplements, or steroid use, but then I saw the mirror." He pointed out the trail of fingerprints and smudges along the glass. "I already made a call to the FBI," Knoll filled them in—he had gotten an e-mail of his own.

Cerova put on gloves and took a closer look at the victim. "I know him. He's a bouncer at 18 is 9."

They hovered over the body, the third in as many days. "What the hell is going on?" Knoll muttered.

"What do the FBI know that we don't?" Cerova added.

Collins, the senior of the group, pulled it together. "It's still our crime scene and we've got a job to do. If the FBI shows up, we can ask them then."

Cerova followed her partner's lead. "Right. Let's go talk to his roommates."

*****

The pitch-black Hellcat pulled up behind the string of squad cars just as they were packing up the coroner's van in the driveway. Martinez put on her game face and exited the vehicle. Huddled in the driveway, Knoll whispered quietly to Cerova, "That's her."

"FBI agent?"

"And possibly the future Mrs. Knoll, but don't tell her that. I want it to be a surprise." He grinned.

Collins appraised Martinez's car, suit, and swagger on the long walk up the street and driveway. A plume of vapor billowed out of her mouth; she even made vaping look cool. "Way out of your league, Doug."

"Never going to knock one out of the park if you don't swing." He grabbed his field bag. "Don't take this the wrong way, but I hope I don't see you guys for a while."

Cerova smiled. "Right back atcha."

Martinez spotted her target from behind her sunglasses; she recognized the ME from yesterday and Detective Cerova from her picture, but the older male next to them was new to her. She nodded at the ME as he walked past and pulled out her ID. "Special Agent Teresa Martinez of the FBI. I'm looking for Detective Jennifer Cerova."

Cerova extended her hand. "That would be me. Nice to meet you, Special Agent Martinez. This is my partner, Detective Marshall Collins." Martinez shook both their hands and elided past the pleasantries. "I understand this scene has similarities to Janice Keller's death?"

"And Emily Schappel's." Cerova took the lead. Martinez slid

her sunglasses off as they entered the house. "Michael Gerrold, age twenty-four. His roommates found him this morning, but time of death was late last night, shortly after returning home from work as a bouncer at 18 is 9," she skirted the edge without overstepping her bounds.

"And the body showed signs of asphyxiation without signs of a struggle?" Martinez inquired as she pulled a pair of gloves out of her pocket.

"Exactly," Collins answered behind her as they made their way to the basement. "As you can see, more fingerprints on the mirror, and it's only a matter of time before our techs confirm they are his."

Cerova looked for any crack in the agent's impassive mien but found none.

Martinez crouched down and examined the mirror at length without touching it. Neither Cerova nor Collins knew what exactly she was looking for, but kept silent until Martinez rose. "And his room?"

The detectives led the way and watched her work under the guise of the Detroit PD making themselves available to the FBI. It was obvious that she was looking for something, but neither of them could suss out what it was or if she had found it. Nonetheless, she was thorough; by the time they left the house, the rest of the uniforms had packed up.

Martinez striped off her gloves and shook their hands again. "Thanks for the call. We would still like to be informed of similar cases, should they occur."

"So, Emily Schappel…?" Cerova asked.

"We have what we need for now," she curtly responded.

"Anything you can tell us that might help us apprehend who is responsible?" Collins inquired.

"I'm not at liberty to speak about an ongoing investigation, but if our efforts pan out, you should have fewer bodies," Martinez answered flatly.

"What about 18 is 9? It seems that all the victims have a connection there," Cerova chimed in.

"As the place where Janice Keller's body was found, we are naturally interested in 18 is 9," Martinez replied diplomatically but said nothing more. A scratchy voice came over the radio on Collins's belt, and he stepped away to answer.

"Duty calls. I won't take up anymore of your time," Martinez made overtures.

"Wait." Cerova stepped in front of her. Despite being five inches shorter than Martinez, her demeanor made up for it. The detective lowered her poker face and candid concern shone through. "I know you can't tell me anything, but my little sister hangs out at 18 is 9. Is she in any danger?"

Martinez paused. "Maybe skip the club scene for a while," she suggested. "And, if the last three crime scenes are any indication, stay away from mirrors." She reached into her pocket. "Shit, I must have left my vape pen inside."

"Jen, we have to go," Collins yelled.

Cerova was torn; she had so many questions and couldn't shake the feeling that Martinez had answers, but she knew it was important if Collins was using her first name. Glomming onto her indecision, Martinez allowed a small chink in her neutral expression and made direct eye contact with the detective. "We are both working for the same goal, just on different paths."

Cerova nodded and headed back to her car where Collins was waiting, while Martinez headed back into the house to conduct her real investigation.

Chapter Fourteen

Detroit, Michigan, USA
6th of August, 2:00 p.m. (GMT-4)

Meridiana lingered in her bath and sipped an Asian pear mimosa, preparing for the inevitable. She loathed the idea of calling home; it never got easier, despite all the time that had passed. Centuries of her surviving—nay, thriving—outside of hell evaporated the second her mother or father answered.

Her siblings were somewhat better; they didn't understand her either but they knew their parents, which made them marginally more tolerable. Whenever any of them were put off by one of their parents' schemes, they would defiantly declare that they were joining her in the mortal realm. Meridiana would summon them through and give them a taste of her non-evil existence among humans; it wouldn't take long before they grew bored and returned to hell, acquiescing to whatever machinations were originally in place.

As tedious as it was babysitting rebelling devils, it was nice to be in the company of beings that just got you, even if you couldn't be evil anymore. No matter how much time she spent among humans, she was still a stranger in a strange land, constantly having to translate herself into mortal existence.

It wasn't that she *wanted* to go back to hell—the banishment was technically a punishment, but some days the burden was lighter than others—but it would be nice to not have to work so hard just to exist.

Meridiana fortified herself in a ritual of her own, starting with a soak in the tub. Once bathed, she cocooned herself in soft terrycloth and started with her hair, sculpting the long black locks into place. Today, she was going rockabilly, an Amy Winehouse sort of vibe. When she was satisfied with the volume of her bump and curls, she started on her face. As a succubus, she was a natural beauty and certainly didn't need help to be attractive. To Meridiana, applying makeup was akin to a warrior girding his loins for battle. Nailing liquid eyeliner on the first try was its own kind of magic. Among devils, clothing was optional. If you were going to wear something, it had to be a power move; otherwise you just came off weak and insecure.

Sitting in front of her vanity, she appraised her work and found it good. She took a sip of another mimosa and stashed it to the side, knowing she would need it afterward. With a deep breath, she summoned her will. Her flawless reflection in the mirror shimmered until it dissipated and a horned devil answered, the small upper claws of her velvety wings peeking just into frame. "Meridiana? Is that you?" a familiar voice called out across the planes.

"Hi Mom," she greeted the regal figure in front of her. "You look well. How's hell?"

"Oh, you know, hot and mercurial." She rolled her eyes and waved dismissively. "I'm thinking it may be time to get away."

Please don't ask to come for a visit! Meridiana prayed to whatever deity was listening. She changed the subject, "How's Dad?"

"Still on a bender! He's been gone for ages, doing who knows what," she tutted.

"You know Dad, he's a regular paterfamilias. He'll turn up eventually, probably with some great stories and grisly trophies," she cajoled her mother.

The devil twisted her mouth. "You're probably right. So what do you want? I know this isn't a social call."

Meridiana didn't bothering denying it; there were only so many times they could have the same argument. "I was calling to ask you about something that happened a long time ago in the mortal realm. I know you used to spend a lot more time here back in the day."

"Before I had all these responsibilities," she sighed. It wasn't easy being one of the consorts of a Great Earl of Hell.

"Do you remember something called the Hollow back in Mesopotamia? Killed a bunch of Sumerians? It would have been big news at the time," Meridiana tried to stir her mother's memory.

"Let me think…. Humans die so fast and easy, it's hard to keep up with what's killing them en masse at any given time," she muttered. "Could you say it again?"

"The Hollow," Meridiana repeated slowly in Sumerian.

"It rings a bell. Something to do with mirrors?" she guessed.

"Yes!" Meridiana exclaimed. "That's it. What do you remember about that?"

"It was chaos! A hungry time for soul eaters. It came from another plane, in through the mirrors and still water," she recounted, enjoying the attention; it wasn't often that someone asked for her knowledge.

"Do you remember how they got rid of it?" Meridiana guided her mother's account.

"They melted down all their mirrors and made some statue—I think they made sacrifices to it. They covered their pots and only drew from moving waters. Common sense, really," she pooh-poohed.

"Do you know anything else about it? Where it came from? What attracts it? Any vulnerabilities?" Meridiana asked.

Her mother stiffened. "Meridiana, you know I don't hold truck with outsiders."

"Yes, Mother," she apologized reflexively.

"Why don't you ever call in your true form? I'm sure you look nice to the mortals, but I miss seeing my pretty poppet," her mother chided. "You had the nicest horns of your brood."

"Going full devil freaks people out, Mom," she tried to explain.

"Well, that's their problem. You come from a long and lofty linage, despite your…affliction." She euphemistically referred to her child's curse to no longer do evil. "You should be proud of who you are and where you come from."

"I'll keep that in mind in the future," Meridiana humored her. "I really have to be going, but it was nice seeing you and I'm sure Dad will be home soon."

The devil curled her wings around her like a cloak. "Take care of yourself, Meridiana."

"You too, Mom." Her mother's visage rippled away and she was left staring back at herself in the form of Leigh Meyer. The succubus leaned back in her chair and picked up her drink. Astral communication was tiring in and of itself, more so considering her interlocutor. Still, she knew more than before.

Outsiders were universally considered weird by everyone and general wisdom was best to avoid them altogether. The closest modern humans came to knowing them were in the tales of Cthulhu, chronicled by an otherwise unambitious, languid man with second sight. She'd had to really work him over to release, both sexually and in his writing, but it was nothing she couldn't handle. Thankfully, he hadn't seen what had become of his work…plush toys, printed fabrics, cartoons, and porn. So much porn. He'd went to the edge of madness to warn humanity, and they fetishized the monsters.

The flutter of movement in the three-panel mirror of her vanity broke her reminiscence. She turned her big brown eyes to the glass and smiled—she had a visitor. She'd spent enough time as the object of desire to know when she was being watched. She pretended not to notice the unseen eyes and feigned a doe-eyed innocence as she fussed with her impeccable hair.

Her right hand reached for the dagger strapped to her thigh. She felt something swirl against her will, tasting her, but before it could figure out that she was not food, Meridiana reached her left hand through the mirror, feeling the sticky cold damp that pressed expectantly against the other side of the glass. She pulled her hand and what it clasped back into the mortal realm, slamming her dagger solidly into the oily appendage. A cry echoed through two realms, and she fed on its psychic pain. It tasted of the sea: salty and full of umami, with a slightly sweet finish. She looked back into the mirror, but the connection had already been severed, leaving part of whatever it was behind.

She went to the kitchen, finished the last of the champagne, and fetched a clean mason jar for the nub and effluvium pinned to the top of her vanity. She washed off her dagger before returning it to its leather sheath and slipped into a sundress. She bent down, fastening the buckle on her wedge sandals, and grabbed her wide-brimmed Dolce & Gabbana sunglasses. After surviving the most recent trial-by-mother, she decided on a riverside stroll and a late lunch.

She slipped the capped mason jar into her purse and pulled out her phone, dialing the number on Special Agent Martinez's card. It picked up on the third ring. "Federal Bureau of Investigations, Special Agent Teresa Martinez's office. How can I help you?"

"This is Leigh Meyer. Special Agent Martinez stopped

by my place earlier this afternoon. Please let her know that I have additional information that could be helpful to her investigation."

Chapter Fifteen

Detroit, Michigan, USA
6th of August, 5:25 p.m. (GMT-4)

Martinez churned over her busy afternoon as she crawled in rush hour traffic. At Gerrold's house, she'd confirmed him as the third known victim of the Hollow, and like Emily Schappel, he wasn't a registered practitioner and there was nothing magical at his house. Then she'd met with Meridiana and took her account on what she'd found out about the Hollow, and the attempted attack afterward. Martinez had never imagined she would be sipping iced tea with a fiend on the riverside with a piece of outsider in her bag, nor had she considered that succubi had mothers...but why not? Everyone had a mother.

According to Meridiana, it had co-opted her reflection in the mirror and made eye contact to entice her to make physical contact with the mirror, which quickly turned against its favor. Not only was she absent a soul—at least in the mortal sense of the word—she had a very sharp dagger and the ability to astrally reach through the mirror. Martinez had picked up on the succubus's indignation; she might no longer kill what she caught, but she was still a hunter, not prey. When asked about the composition of her dagger, Meridiana "hadn't the foggiest" and ordered dessert.

It had been the best lead Martinez had on the killer in the past two days, but she still had her doubts about working with a devil. Clearly, Meridiana could lie, as evidenced by her statement to Detroit PD about the nature of her relationship with Janice Keller, which piqued Martinez's interest.

She'd returned to the Salt Mine and spent a few hours on the sixth floor, first catching up Chloe and Dot in hopes they would know what could be done with the contents of the mason jar. A judicious salting had confirmed it was the same being responsible for the three asphyxiated bodies in the morgue, but other than that, Martinez was outclassed. Outsiders were rarely encountered compared to all the other types of supernatural creatures, and were therefore only briefly touched upon during her training.

Martinez would have read up on them except those were the exact same volumes that the twins would need to conduct their research. While the twins had eidetic memories, being able to physically manipulate the information made it much easier for them to make connections, rather than doing it all in their minds' eyes. So instead of reading about outsiders, Martinez had spent an hour reading up on Meridiana's history, which turned out to be quite convoluted. She was a succubus whose favored pre-curse pastime was enticing religious people to break their vows of celibacy, but she ended up falling in love with Gerbert of Aurillac, a brilliant, progressive scholar who'd fled to a religious life after getting his own heart broken. Gerbert's meteoric rise to become the first French Pope in 999 was controversial; his broad scope of learning from "the heathens" in mathematics and astronomy was treated with suspicion, say nothing of the rumors of sorcery and consorting with the devil—a popular claim made against political rivals in religious power structures at the time, except it happened to be true in this case.

There was a long and—at least to Martinez—largely pedantic argument about the curse's order of operation: was is only the curse that had allowed her to fall in love for the first time, or was it the act of a devil falling in love that had cursed her? Either way, Meridiana's cover had been blown and she was banished from hell, no longer able to do evil. With her name plastered all over the incident, she became famous and her normally power-laden true name flittered on the lips of every would-be summoner in Europe. However, the curse had removed the power from her name, lest someone used it to compel her to do evil and therefore circumvent the curse; apparently, whatever force had cursed her was well aware of the existence of rules lawyers. Since then, Meridiana had assumed different forms and names over time and the library had incomplete records on her activities, except for the occasional reference that speculatively attributed some activity to her influence.

When Martinez had questioned Chloe and Dot on how reliable Meridiana could be, they seemed realistic but untroubled—after all, not being evil wasn't the same as being good. They'd rationalized it this way: if her information panned out, it saved them time and effort; if it didn't, that would have become evident through the research and investigation that would have had to happen anyway. While summoning something to confirm the information regarding the outsider was an option, it would have to be something old, powerful, definitely evil, and done at a high cost. There would be the power of the pact and the security of the summoning circle to fall back on, but it was still a gamble because magic always was. Plus, no one relished the idea of a fiend having the taste of their blood in its mouth. Either way, they'd had work to do and shooed her out of their library.

After that, Martinez had made a pit stop in Weber's workshop and found him in a state. Not only had he put the mirror back together, but he had figured out that the puukko was in fact an astral blade, extremely rare as the astral plane was mostly insubstantial. He'd nodded affirmatively when Martinez informed him they were dealing with an outsider, and told her about the magical residue that lingered in the mirror. According to Weber, if Keller's ritual or spell had weakened the barrier between the mortal realm and whatever outer plane the Hollow resided in, contact with the astral blade could have effectively created a stable shortcut between the two.

Martinez had thanked him for his work, even though she wasn't exactly sure what to do with it. When she'd asked if it was reversible, Weber seemed doubtful—Keller had already tried breaking the mirror without effect. Nonetheless, he'd promised to look into the matter.

After running the information in her head yet again one more time, Martinez finally reached her destination and pulled into the now-empty parking lot of 18 is 9. She examined herself in the small vanity mirror and did her best to look less governmental: hair down, top two buttons of her blouse undone, cuffs rolled to three-quarters sleeve. She would have liked to have ditched the jacket, but she couldn't without also abandoning her concealed Glock, and that wasn't an option. She cut off the engine and stepped out of her car, adopting a lighter persona as she approached the barred entrance.

She banged on the door until she heard someone within yelling for her to hold her horses. The club wasn't scheduled to open for another couple of hours, and with any luck, not even then. A sliding slot opened and a pair of brown eyes peered through. "We're closed. Come back later," someone barked through the hole.

She smiled sweetly and touched her hair. "I'm here to talk to Aloysius. We had such a nice time last night that he told me I could stop by anytime. Could you tell him Teresa is here?"

He grunted, "Wait here." The slot closed, and she could hear the commotion behind the door without making out any of the words. A few minutes later, a burly figure opened the door wide for her entry and closed and locked it behind her. "Mr. Hardwick is in his office," he explained as he escorted her through the main floor deep into the back. The club was so different without the lights, music, and people, poignantly empty like Bourbon Street early Sunday morning, after the revelers had retired but before the street cleaners had made their rounds.

They stopped at a door and the bouncer knocked and waited for his boss's "Come in" before opening the solid oak door. The whole of the office came into view, including Hardwick rising to his feet and coming around from the other side of the desk. "Teresa!" he exclaimed, clasping her shoulders and giving her a kiss on each cheek—partly to keep up appearances, partly for selfish reasons. "Take a seat. Can I get you anything to drink?"

She played along and returned his Continental greeting. "Just water today," she answered.

"Bottle of water for the lady." He dismissed her escort and sat back down behind the desk. "To what do I owe the pleasure?"

"I'm here to ask you not to open 18 is 9 tonight," she stated bluntly. "You didn't hear this from me, but since Janice's murder, Detroit PD has found two more bodies of people that had been to 18 is 9 shortly before their deaths. It appears that whatever killed Janice could be using the club to pick its prey."

Hardwick cheerful facade disappeared. "Who are the other

two victims? Were they magicians?"

"I don't think so. Do the names Emily Schappel and Michael Gerrold mean anything to you?" Martinez replied.

Hardwick gasped. "Not Michael—he was just working last night!" His shock seemed genuine, and Martinez took note that he not only immediately knew the name of one of his bouncers, but his work schedule as well. Either he was more than just another piece of muscle, or Hardwick regarded those in his employment as more than just staff.

"I'm afraid so. Do you know of any connection they had with Janice? Maybe closet practitioners?" Martinez knew not everyone registered with the Salt Mine.

His ashen face shook side to side. "No. I don't even know this Emily person. Do you have a picture?" The door opened again and the wall of muscle handed Martinez a bottle of water before retreating. Martinez pulled up a photo of the blonde on her phone and turned it around for Hardwick to examine. He shook his head. "She wasn't a regular."

He poured himself a drink from the side cabinet behind him while Martinez recovered her phone. She unscrewed the bottle's cap and took a sip of water to give him time to process. "Look," she started gently, "I know we don't know each other very well and I know it's a lot to ask on a hunch, but I get the impression that you pride yourself on making this a safe space for people that are…differently aligned than the rest of society. If I'm right, every night you stay open is putting more people at risk." She caught his attention and held eye contact. "Give me some time to get a plan together."

Hardwick rolled the amber liquid around in his tumbler. "How much time are we talking about?"

"At least two or three days. I've got a lot of irons in the fire and something should pan out," Martinez replied tactically. It was a short enough time to seem like a reasonable request, and if need be, it would be easier to keep it shut once he'd agreed to not open to begin with.

"Are my personal staff safe?" he asked, fully aware potential predators included supernatural creatures.

"We think its using mirrors in its attack, and your place is covered with them." She feigned reluctance at revealing case information—if he was half the gossip she'd suspected he was, the news would be out among the magical community in no time. "I would cover all the mirrors with cloth, to be on the safe side. Tell them you are doing some cleaning or thinking about remodeling," she suggested.

He found her ease with believable lies both attractive and alarming. "Anything you can do to keep the Detroit PD off my back?" he inquired.

She shook her head. "I'll do what I can, but I can't grab jurisdiction on all these murders and if I caution them to stay away, it will only make them more curious and determined to get at you."

He finished his drink and sat back in his oversized chair.

"So you're basically asking me to take a financial hit and fend off a police investigation on my own," he summed up gruffly.

She mimicked his posture. "I'm asking you to help me protect people and do what you do best: lawyer up and appear available without actually answering any questions," she called his bluff.

He couldn't stop the smile of appreciation from creeping at the corners of his mouth—*oh, she was good*. "And you'll let me know as soon as it's safe to open again?"

"I'll toast reopening night with you," she reassured him. "And Aloysius, *try* to sound surprised when the cops do finally come around?"

He smirked at her bravado.

Chapter Sixteen

Detroit, Michigan, USA
6th of August, 6:23 p.m. (GMT-4)

Mira slung her messenger bag for work over her shoulder and juggled the bags of groceries she had picked up on her way to Jenny's. They had eaten a lot of take-out the past couple nights and she toyed with the idea of cooking dinner. Plus, someone had to replenish the ice cream supply. She fished her keys out of her pocket and called out as she opened the door.

"I'm home, Jenny!" she announced as she made a beeline for the kitchen. "Sorry I'm a little late. I stopped by the store on the way home. How does dinner *not* out of a foil wrapper sound?" Mira continued shouting as she unpacked the cold items; she could not let the ice cream melt—oh the humanity! A muffled yell came from deeper in the house, but Mira couldn't make out what was said. "I can't understand you. Hold on, I'm coming to you." She pulled out a cold beer and popped the cap with the church key on her key ring.

Mira wove through the living room toward Jenny's bedroom and found her older sister in the bathroom, nailing bolts of black fabric across the mirror. She lowered the beer from her lips. "What on earth are you doing?"

Jenny put the last nail in with a solid blow of the hammer and took the beer from her sister's hand. "How'd you know this is what I needed?" she teased and took a swig before handing it back. "It's a precautionary measure, a tip from the FBI," she answered cryptically.

"The FBI told you to cover your bathroom mirror?" she asked incredulously.

"No, someone told me it wouldn't be a bad idea to stay away from mirrors, and I'm not committed enough to the idea to actually remove the mirrors from the house," Jenny replied, gathering her tools. "Give me a hand; I still have to do the one in bathroom by your room."

Jenny was trying to keep the mood light, and Mira's intuition kicked in. "Did you find another body?"

"Mira, you know I can't talk about ongoing investigations," Jenny responded and hated how much she sounded like Special Agent Martinez at that moment.

Mira shrugged. "So you can't talk about it, but I can still make speculations based on your actions. You found another body, it's got a connection with 18 is 9 and something to do with mirrors, and that's why you're acting crazy like Grandma Rosellini."

"Hey, I'm still your older sister. Show some respect," Jenny yipped back, handing her the bolt of fabric still wrapped around cardboard while she carried the tools.

"Remember when Grandpa died? She did the same thing—

covered all the mirrors in the house so his spirit wouldn't get trapped," Mira elaborated to illustrate her point as she dutifully followed her sister. Jenny climbed on the countertop, grabbed her hammer, and put a few nails in her mouth. Mira handed her the edge of the fabric and took a seat on the lip of the tub while Jenny secured the first corner. "So, who was it? Anyone I know?"

"Mira, I can't tell you until the name is released. Their family has a right to know first," Jenny answered softly.

Mira read her sister like a book. "It's someone I know, isn't it? Is it Sheryl? Connie? Tracy?" she started running through names at a lightning pace.

"Who said it was a woman?" Jenny mumbled through the nails in her mouth.

"It's not Aloysius, is it?!" Mira exclaimed.

Jenny sighed and climbed off the counter. She put her tools down and sat on the toilet lid opposite Mira. She knew she should wait until it hit the news, but she'd heard Collins speaking to the deceased's parents on the phone as she was walking out of the precinct. "It's Michael Gerrold."

Utter shock hit Mira's face. "What?! How?" Fat tears welled in her eyes.

Jenny put her sister's head against her shoulder and rubbed her back. "I don't know yet and I can't go into specifics, but I promise, this is different than the time Grandma Rosellini made us sleep with grated onions in our socks when we had colds."

After a few minutes Mira cried herself out and unrolled some toilet paper to blow her nose. "Are we in danger? Is that what this is about?"

Jenny shrugged her shoulders and answered honestly, "I don't know, but if covering the mirrors helps, I'll do it."

Mira dried her eyes with the back of her hand. "Let me give you a hand," she offered, and held up the fabric while Jenny nailed it into the drywall. "You know we're going to look a mess without mirrors."

"So we'll embrace our curls and go au naturale for a little while." Jenny packed everything away. "Don't act like you don't do your makeup in the car on the way to work half the time." She gave her younger sister her super judgy face.

"It's better than texting and driving," Mira deflected.

"Being less bad is not the same as being good," Jenny commented and wandered into the kitchen. The counter was covered in a hodgepodge of fresh produce, ground beef, pasta, cheeses, and a nice loaf of bread. "So what's for dinner?"

"I was thinking baked ziti with garlic bread." Mira grabbed an apron; she felt so adult making a proper dinner for her older sister. "I even bought a bottle of red wine on sale, but I'm not sure if it's any good," she confessed.

Jenny pulled two goblets from the cabinet and a wine opener from a drawer. "Only one way to find out. If it sucks, we'll make chicken marsala later this week."

Chapter Seventeen

Detroit, Michigan, USA
6th of August, 7:00 p.m. (GMT-4)

Martinez opened her front door and ran straight to the kitchen for some water to quench her thirst. She checked the app on her phone: three and a half miles in twenty-nine minutes. She secured the keyless deadbolt on the front door before stretching out and hitting her calves, quads, hamstrings, and IT bands on her foam roller. She kicked off her shoes, lay flat on her back, and stared at the ceiling of her living room.

The physical exertion had given her mind time to unwind and make sense of all the information swirling around in there. It had taken years for her to figure out that the best cure for mental congestion was to get some distance from it; her natural inclination was to keep banging her head against the same cerebral wall until she broke through to the other side. Now, she knew better; she exercised, ran some errands, cooked something, zoned out on mindless media, slept on it…anything that allowed her thoughts to finish percolating into something usable. Unfortunately, she hadn't had any epiphanies on her run, but she found clarity of purpose with an actionable list of things to help move forward.

Martinez reluctantly left Dead Man's Pose and headed

upstairs. Once in her bedroom, she stripped off her drenched clothing; while the heat of the day had started to dissipate, it was still quite warm outside. She passed her covered mirrors and turned on the taps for a tepid shower, letting the water beat down on her. She'd been pretty sure that outsiders were covered by the wards in place, but Wilson was on vacation and she didn't want to bother him when covering the mirrors would do. After all, Janice Keller wasn't killed in her home.

She toweled off and dressed into her pajamas: an oversized t-shirt and a pair of cotton boxers. Enough time had passed since her run that her appetite had returned with a vengeance. She rummaged through the fridge for leftovers and created a pot roast salad with a ripe plum for dessert, checking her e-mail between bites. As Knoll had promised, her inbox contained the coroner's reports on Janice Keller and Emily Schappel, as well as the lab report on the substance found in both their lungs: organic substance unknown, closest corollary hagfish slime. Having no idea what that meant, she went to the internet and immediately was glad that she'd finished eating. After the third or fourth hagfish video, she felt that she'd gotten the gist and moved on.

The next message was from the FBI: IT had cracked open Keller's phone and laptop, and both were waiting for her at her office. Now that Keller's death had been officially assigned to her, she could avail herself of the FBI's resources and take the time for a more thorough search of Keller's house. It was a balancing act, being FBI Special Agent Martinez and Salt Mine

Agent Lancer; sometimes it felt like she was working solo at two jobs. She was still figuring out how to take advantage of the resources available to her while making sure the left hand didn't know what the right was doing. Obviously, stopping the deaths was her first priority, but it was all a little too neat for Martinez's taste—how does a practitioner like Keller get her hands on a ritual to contact an outsider with an astral dagger on standby?

Once she cleared out her inbox, Martinez put in a request for the Salt Mine analysts to look for unsolved murders with a cause of death of asphyxiation: mechanism unknown in the past two months and keep a watch for new deaths with the same COD. She had been operating under the assumption that Keller was the Hollow's first victim and that the killings were localized to Detroit, but she had forgotten one of the cardinal rules of investigation: question everything you think you know. If it's true, it would hold up to scrutiny.

Martinez made some Sleepytime tea, taking time to smile at the drowsy bear in a cap and gown on the box, and took stock of where she stood. She knew what was killing people, she knew how it was doing it, but she didn't know how to stop it from killing more people short of getting rid of all the mirrors everywhere. She knew it was early days in the case, but four attacks in three days did not convey the sense that time was on her side. There were substantially more people and more mirrors around than in the times of ancient Sumer.

She picked up her phone and pulled up her contacts.

Dialing JL, she heard a familiar voice pick up on the second ring. "Hello?"

"Hey Joan. It's Teresa. From work," Martinez inserted awkwardly. The background noise sounded like she was watching TV.

"Oh hey," Liu answered, pausing her program. "What's up?"

"You got a second to talk? I need to run something by you."

"Sure, give me a second," she replied, leaving the couch and mouthing apologies to her guest. She moved to another room and closed the door. "Okay, shoot."

Martinez sunk into her couch and asked in resignation, "When do you call for a situation room?"

"If you're asking, you probably need to make the call," Liu advised.

"But I don't want to be the boy that cried wolf," she griped.

"What parameters are pulling you in that direction?" Her careful wording suggested to Martinez that she wasn't completely alone.

"Three deaths in three days by a soul-eating outsider that hasn't been active since ancient history," Martinez summarized concisely.

Liu paused. "Confirmed?"

"Yup."

"Shit," Liu muttered.

Martinez immediately felt better. "So I'm not overreacting?" she verified.

"I'd say not. Have you gone to the Library?" Liu asked, layering her tone with subtext.

"Chloe and Dot are still researching and have even recruited Weber into the effort." Martinez sipped her honey-sweetened herbal tea.

Liu sighed. "It's your call, but I'd wait until they hit a wall. You can always raise the flag if something doesn't smell right or if the situation escalates precipitously."

Martinez nodded her head. "Thanks. I just needed to know I wasn't making a mountain out of a molehill."

"Any precautions I should be taking?" Liu inquired.

"I covered all the mirrors in my house earlier tonight," Martinez answered.

"Messaged received," she replied. "And a bit of unsolicited advice? If you pull the trigger, bring food. Everyone likes to eat for free, and these things can go long. Low blood sugar flatters no one," her voice menaced.

Martinez chuckled. "Got it. Sorry to interrupt your evening. Have a good night."

"You too." Liu signed off.

Chapter Eighteen

Detroit, Michigan, USA
7th of August, 8:45 a.m. (GMT-4)

Martinez drank her breakfast protein smoothie while thumbing through Keller's phone: opening her apps, scrolling through the contact list, scanning the texts and direct messages, flipping through photos and videos. The financial apps were password protected, but everything else was not, including her e-mail and journaling app. Most of her e-mails were work-related, billing notifications, or newsletters that Keller had subscribed to spanning a broad range of topics. A quick glance at the inbox revealed so much minutia about Keller's life: where she shopped, banked, and worked out, which charities she supported, which utility companies she used. Her journal entries were few and infrequent, mostly in personal shorthand, and the last entry was over six months ago about getting in better shape.

She flipped over to the calendar where Keller dutifully entered in all her meetings for work, as well as social engagements. Martinez saw "Stephen's birthday party" slotted for ten days ago, a spate of evening events held at her library, and going father back, late-night engagements with LM that stopped around five weeks ago. It lent creditability to Meridiana's account and she was telling the truth about one thing: Keller hadn't been scheduled to see her the night of her death.

There was no sign of Emily Schappel or Michael Gerrold in all the usual places, and Martinez scrolled through pictures until her eyes blurred. She took a break from the small screen and moved to her still-warm coffee and Keller's laptop. While phones were undoubtedly important to people, in Martinez's experience, anything that got saved onto their computers were the things that were precious to them, and for some, there was a slew of work that only happened on computer—not everything can be accomplished with a swipe or tap of a thumb.

Poking around a computer's directory was like getting a glimpse into someone's mind. Not just their interests, but how they thought—how they organized and named things, where they drew categorical lines, and how they made sense of all the information they deemed meaningful at some point in time. Martinez went down the rabbit hole, unraveling the nested folders of Keller's laptop. To her surprise, Keller's tax folder actually contained her taxes and her porn folder was clearly marked—this was not a person who shared her computer with anyone. A peek at her 1040 et al was illuminating; Keller pulled in a decent salary, but her income from investments and sizable nest egg was even more impressive. *It paid to be in divination*, Martinez mused.

Her phone buzzed on the desk and she recognized the number. "Martinez," she answered.

LaSalle's voice came over the line. "Good morning, Agent Martinez. I tried contacting your office but couldn't get through." His inflection intimated her *other* office with the intercom box on one corner of her desk.

"Yeah, I'm at the FBI looking through Keller's phone and laptop," she responded. "What's up?"

"I'm calling to inform you that the sixth floor has come up with a plan and Leader has approved it," he replied. "Details are being sent to your phone as we speak. There's no need to stop by the Mine; Agent Liu will bring the necessary tools before rendezvousing with you at 11:00 a.m. Dress for the country and pack a generous picnic for two. You're going into the Magh Meall."

Martinez composed herself. "Thanks for the heads up."

"No problem," he said casually. "Have fun. There's nothing like your first time."

Martinez pulled up the message as soon as he hung up. She had GPS coordinates located in the Sumpter Township, less than an hour southwest of Detroit, and a time—apparently, that constituted as "details." She packed everything up and took the electronics with her, heading back home to get ready.

She vacillated between excitement and anxiety on the drive and fought the urge to text Liu for more information. Of all the freaky things she'd studied to become a Salt Mine agent, the

Magh Meall was one of the nicer ones. It was supposed to be a heartbreakingly beautiful place where time passed differently and magic could be performed with no karmic cost. Literally the "middle lands" in the tongue of the fae, it was one of the few planes humans could travel to, albeit with restrictions. The gateway for mortal entry was only open an hour after high noon local time, provided that certain rituals and magics were performed.

Even though it was the bridge between the land of fae and the mortal realm, all manner of creatures lived there, not just faeries and humans that wandered in after lunch. Well, all except fiends—fae had a serious hate on for devils and demons. Despite its beauty, it wasn't all fun and games. Mostly old-growth forest, there were real dangers lurking in the Magh Meall, which was why it was best to go in pairs, especially for new agents. More experienced ones could go solo if needs must, but it was not advised.

The first thing Martinez did when she got home was secure Keller's electronics for later inspection. She raided her kitchen for picnic supplies, grabbing fruit, bottled water, a bottle of juice, and some chips; she would have to hit the grocery store on the way out of town. There were two hard and fast rules of the Magh Meall for humans: don't eat or drink anything when you're there and don't take anything out of the Magh Meall back into the mortal realm—the karmic backlash was large and immediate.

She hung up her work clothes for another wear, considering she had been in them less than three hours, and considered what to wear. Neither LaSalle nor the message had said anything about meeting fae, and if Martinez was bringing her gun, she might as well wear jeans, metal be damned. She also brought her focus rosary and wore her periapt—she had yet to encounter a faerie and loaded for bear.

She loaded her car with the meager groceries she had and made eyes on the blanket she kept in the trunk in case she got stranded in winter; it would suffice for a picnic. After a fill up, she stopped by the store and loaded up in the pre-made food section: wraps, sandwiches, potato salad, macaroni salad, and more bottled water. Next, she hit the cookie aisle and grabbed some Highland shortbread. Technically, any crumbled sweet cookie would have worked, but she decided to stick with proper tradition for her first foray.

With the coordinates entered into her phone, Martinez drove out of town. One of the Salt Mine's holdings included some farmland just outside of the city with a greenhouse and a forested patch. Fresh produce aside, it gave local agents a secluded place nearby to enter the Magh Meall.

Martinez spotted Liu inside her car and pulled the Hellcat beside it; she was fifteen minutes early, but still late to the party. Both women exited their vehicles at the same time and started unpacking their gear. "Ready for a picnic?" Liu asked as she hoisted a cooler from her trunk.

"I thought I was bringing the food?" Martinez inquired.

"Goodies packed with salt. It's heavier than sin. Mind grabbing the trench shovel?" Liu slung another bag across her body.

Martinez grabbed the blanket, groceries, and the digging tool. "What about the mirror in the back seat?"

"Leave it," she commanded. "I'll come back for it once we've picked a good spot."

They trekked into the wooded area until they could no longer see their cars before Liu stopped. "Good enough for government work," she quipped, as both agents unburdened themselves of all their gear.

Martinez spread the blanket on the ground, folding it over to make the smallest area needed for the two of them and their gear—$2\pi R$ and all that. She picked up the shovel and started making the trench while Liu retrieved the rest of the ritual components from her car: a three-foot-tall oval mirror, a carriage clock that chimed the hour, a compass, four candles in sturdy holders, and shortbread, just in case Martinez had forgotten.

Liu peeked inside the grocery bag. "Pre-made sandwiches?" she commented with a hint of derision.

"Hey, it's from the chichi grocery store. If you want homemade, you have to give me more than two hours' notice," Martinez huffed as she stepped on the back of the head and cut another section of the shallow trough encircling the blanket.

"You want to fill me in on the plan?"

Liu carefully extracted Keller's repaired mirror from the salt and kept it covered in fabric. "I got the abbreviated version, but essentially, the brains have come up with a scheme to short circuit the connection between the outer plane and the mortal realm by tossing the ritual mirror into the astral plane."

"Be undone by what created it?" Martinez speculated.

"That, or shift one of the endpoints of the connection. I'm a little fuzzy on the theory, but I figured it was too pretty outside to be cooped up underground. That was before I knew the caliber of the menu," Liu gently ribbed her.

"Why don't I finish setup and you finish the circle," Martinez suggested and held out the trenching tool.

Liu took her turn at digging while Martinez drank some water and consulted the compass. At each cardinal direction, she placed a candle in its holder and lit it. Next, she whacked the heel of her hand against the packet of shortbread Liu had brought—no use destroying the nice brand she had bought. "What do you want: brie and ham or roast beef and havarti? I also bought wraps: turkey and swiss, I think?"

"I'll take the ham," Liu answered, completing the circle. She leaned the tool against a nearby tree and entered the circle, gladly accepting a bottle of water and a seat in the shade. Martinez then distributed a line of crumbled shortbread inside the circle.

They ate and drank their fill, going over the operation in

detail. If everything went according to plan, they shouldn't be long in the Magh Meall, but it was never a good idea to enter the middle lands the least bit hungry or thirsty.

At five till noon, they started a simple chant of supplication to the fae until the carriage clock chimed twelve times. Silence fell over the two women as they ended their song and closed their eyes. Each summoned their will and wound it around the trench, starting at the bottom and working its way up until they were encased in an invisible dome of collective magical energy. After an hour of quiet meditation, the carriage clock chimed thirteen times, and the women found themselves in the Magh Meall.

Even before Martinez opened her eyes, she knew she was somewhere *other*; she had no idea that air could smell so pure and crisp. Even the dirt smelled clean. Liu breathed it in deeply. "I love the Magh Meall," she said dreamily. Martinez opened her eyes to the endless forest surrounding them on all sides. The massive trunks hummed with life and their broad canopy only allowed streaks of the purple-tinged light to touch the ground. Small wildflowers bloomed in patches, in colors that were more vivid than any hue Martinez had ever seen. She bent down and caressed the soft velvety petals. Now she understood the temptation to bring home a souvenir—it was the most perfect flower she had ever experienced.

Liu watched Martinez process the sensory overload that was the Magh Meall. "Work first, then play." Liu sighed, as much for her own benefit as Martinez's. "You know how to access the astral plane?"

"Academically speaking, yes, but I've never actually cast it," Martinez qualified.

Liu shrugged her shoulders. "Ain't no better teacher than experience."

Martinez pulled out her rosary and held one of the large beads between her fingers, just in case her spell needed a little oomph. She dipped into her well and shaped her will into a ball; it felt different than it did in the mortal realm. Normally it felt dense, like a baseball. In the Magh Meall, it felt airy and light, like a puff of meringue. Her voice echoed among the trees as she started her incantation. She fed it more will, like rolling up spun sugar around a stick, until it held so much energy that Martinez could no longer hold it back. She released her will and shot it through the three-foot-tall oval mirror, opening the threshold into the astral plane.

"Easy killer…" Liu chuckled. "It's a good thing nothing lives there, because you could have taken its head off."

"Magic goes a lot farther here, doesn't it?" Martinez commented.

"Well, it is part fae," Liu conceded and nudge the covered mirror toward Martinez. "You want to do the honors?"

Martinez lifted Keller's repaired mirror and slipped off the cloth. The tessellated blue and white tiles gleamed and the glass caught a beam of light. *Hail Mary, full of grace…* Martinez hurled it into the large oval mirror and watched it fly through the glass. She then reached out and touched the surface of oval mirror, closing the gateway—the astral plane was a place mortals could access in the Magh Meall but not enter.

"So it is done." Liu laid the mirror flat. "You wanna take a short walk?"

"Isn't it dangerous?" Martinez asked.

"So is wandering the mortal realms, but we do that every day. And there is no place in Detroit as pretty as this." Liu pulled out a ball of yarn and tied a surgeon's knot to the loop of a metal stake. With a firm step, she planted it into the ground inside the circle. "Come on, we have a hundred yards. How much trouble can we get into?"

*****

Martinez couldn't remember the last time she'd played hooky, but since time passed differently in the Magh Meall, it was only 1:15 p.m. when she and Liu returned to the mortal realm with one less mirror. Famished from their frolicking, they'd devoured the remains of the picnic, including the Highland shortbread, before packing up and heading back to town. Liu had agreed to take everything back to the Salt Mine, giving Martinez time to make a more thorough search of Keller's house.

Armed with her saltcaster, plenty of fine salt, her badge,

and jurisdiction, Martinez tore Keller's house apart, determined to find out how the librarian knew the ritual that started this whole business. Martinez had broken it down in her head: if it was intentional, Keller was either the sole perpetrator that somehow acquired the directions, or a willing co-conspirator of someone with a lot more esoteric knowledge. However, given that she'd called in the tip to the Salt Mine, Martinez was more inclined to believe it was accidental or that she was an unwitting pawn that blew the whistle as soon as she'd figured out what she'd done.

After four hours, Martinez called it quits and returned home, empty-handed but not defeated—she still hadn't finished going through Keller's laptop. With the music turned up from the living room, she danced around the kitchen, making toast, frying two eggs, and microwaving roasted vegetables and pot roast with gravy—creativity was the soul of repurposing leftovers. Fueled up, Martinez spent the next few hours combing through Keller's laptop, looking through her files, browsing her bookmarked sites on the net, and seeing what Janice Keller got into on her downtime. Somewhere between the long day, the full belly, and the glow of the screen, Martinez fell asleep on her couch.

She was startled when the ringing of her phone woke her, not only at the late hour—2:54 a.m.—but the fact she wasn't in bed and was still in her jeans. There were a limited pool of numbers set to override her phone's do not disturb hours, so she knew she had to take it. "This is Martinez," she answered.

"This is a call for Special Agent Martinez of the FBI," the crisp female voice on the other line stated. "You have a series of messages from a Detective Cerova of Detroit PD. The detective was quite insistent that these messages be brought to your attention immediately, as she has found three more bodies that might interest you."

She sat up abruptly and caught movement out of the corner of her eye—the silent little one of her ghostly roommates was running through down the hall into the kitchen, no doubt joining Wolfhard and Millie. They usually stayed in the attic, but sometimes wandered the house at night when Martinez was usually asleep in her room. All grogginess was gone with the spike of adrenaline.

"Did she give you an address or phone number?" Martinez asked as she grabbed a pen and hastily scribbled the information on a notepad. After repeating it back to make sure she'd transcribed it correctly, she ended the call and went into the kitchen.

"Hello, Teresa," Millie greeted her. "You're up awfully late. I hope we didn't wake you."

"No, I fell asleep doing work and just got a call," Martinez reassured the kind spectral woman. She grabbed her gear and keys. "I'll be out for a bit. Watch the house for me while I'm gone?"

Wolfhard materialized next to Millie and removed the

ethereal pipe from his mouth. "Of course. You be careful out there."

Martinez smiled. "I will, but the things that go bump in the night should be afraid of me." She locked the door behind her, and the trio heard the sound of the Hellcat's engine turn over from the kitchen. Wolfhard continued his smoke while Millie worked on needlework and the little one played with her dolly.

Chapter Nineteen

Detroit, Michigan, USA
8th of August, 8:40 a.m. (GMT-4)

Martinez had never been to the conference room on the fourth floor of the Salt Mine. The meeting didn't start until 9:00 a.m., but she came early to prepare. It was her first situation room, and she didn't want to botch it. She had taken Liu's suggestion and brought donuts and muffins, a box of coffee, and a couple cartons of juice—hopefully it wouldn't run into lunch.

She stared down the length of the oblong table and the empty high-backed chairs. She took a sip of her coffee and claimed a seat near the front of the room; as lead agent, she was responsible for presenting the case. Martinez started writing out key points on the whiteboard and pinning up pictures with magnets. It was the first supernatural murder board she had set up, but the process was remarkably similar to the mundane version.

She had spent the wee hours of the night confirming all three bodies were the Hollow's victims, and that their deaths occurred after she and Liu had returned from the Magh Meall. 18 is 9 had been closed all night and none of them were employees. With the body count doubling overnight, she'd little choice but to phone the Mine and put in the request for a situation room meeting. A situation room was an agent's "In case of fire, break glass." When your case took a turn for the worse and you were having problems with containment, it was all hands on deck to figure out a solution and fix it. It brought in Leader, Chloe and Dot, Weber, and all available agents to focus on the problem at hand, but Martinez wasn't sure what to expect, considering she had already availed herself to the librarians and their quartermaster.

With everything set up, Martinez left the room to stretch her legs and calm her nerves, and nearly ran headlong into LaSalle in the hall. His large hands instinctually reached out and touched her shoulder, stopping her advance abruptly.

"I'm so sorry!" she apologized in a fit of embarrassment. "Did I get any coffee on you?"

LaSalle checked his suit. "Nope, you're in the clear," he answered. "Do you need something for the meeting?"

Martinez threw out a suggestion, "Maybe a valium?"

LaSalle chuckled. "Sadly, we don't stock it in the supply room."

She smirked. "Answer's never 'yes' if you don't ask. I'm just going to take a lap and clear my head. Hovering isn't going to make people show up sooner."

LaSalle nodded knowingly. "For what it's worth, it takes a lot of balls to call a situation room, and I know of at least one former agent that might still be with us if they had made the call instead of thinking they could tackle things alone."

"Thanks," she replied, and gave him a genuine smile before they proceeded in opposite directions. She locked her travel mug—perhaps more caffeine was not what she needed. On her second lap, Martinez stopped by the bathroom for a pit stop. As she washed her hands, she checked her appearance; it was challenging fixing your hair and doing your makeup without a big mirror, but she had managed all right, all things considered. She took a deep breath and stared at herself in the glass, unafraid of encountering the Hollow with the Salt Mine's exhaustive defenses. "You've got this," she told herself before checking her watch and heading back to the conference room.

Chloe and Dot were sitting in their specially made chair for two, and Weber was looking over the pictures hanging on her murder board. Liu was helping herself to refreshments with Nalin Buchholz—codename Hobgoblin. Martinez ran her eyes over the agent; at 6'3" and 185 pounds, he was lean muscle wrapped in light mocha skin. He would have been devastatingly attractive if he wasn't such an ass about it; for Martinez, personality went a long way. She didn't know anything about his background and she honestly couldn't remember ever seeing him at his assigned office on the fifth floor, but if you needed to blow something up, Hobgoblin was your man. Leader had given him the codename because of his proclivity toward destruction, and he embodied that quality so much that when the other agents thought about him, he was not Nalin nor Buchholz—he was Hobgoblin. Martinez smiled and greeted everyone while she took her seat.

A few minutes passed when a boisterous "Good morning!" broke the reserved silence. All eyes went to the doorway as a petite blonde dressed in Givenchy with matching accessories strolled into the conference room. She lowered her voice conspiratorially, "I hear we have a situation."

"Alicia! What on earth on you doing here? Not that it isn't a pleasure to see you," Buchholz recovered first and kissed her outstretched hand.

Moncrief—codename Clover—motioned for Hobgoblin to pour her some juice as she took off her gloves and settled them in her bag. "I was in town on other business when Leader sent out the message. I figured I might as well stop by and warm the seat in the office for a change." Heiress Alicia Elspeth Hovdenak Moncrief didn't have aliases or clock in like the other Salt Mine agents, so the routine seemed downright novel.

"I appreciate you coming in. This case could use a dose of good luck," Martinez commented aloud, reserving *and the resources of old magic and money* to herself. With the ice broken, smaller conversations picked up across the room until Leader entered at exactly 9:00 a.m., dressed in jeans, a cream linen blouse, and an azure cable sweater vest she'd knitted herself. Despite her relaxed appearance, the indomitable will of the salt-and-pepper-haired woman silenced the room and effectively called the meeting to order. LaSalle shut the door from the outside.

Leader announced that the other agents were indisposed and that they should begin. Martinez quickly ran over the case to make sure everyone was on the same page. She was glad she'd made the board as a visual reference, as some were clearly not as steeped in standard investigative procedure as she was.

"Which brings us to yesterday," she concluded the beginning of the conundrum. "Agent Liu and I executed the sixth-floor plan of throwing the mirror Keller used to contact the outsider into the astral plane. However, the killings have not stopped. In fact, they have increased and are no longer bound to the 18 is 9 connection. The body count is now up to six in five days, three of those in the past twelve hours. While I've secured jurisdiction of Keller's death, local law enforcement is investigating the other five. And that is where we stand."

Martinez sat down, yielding the floor to Chloe. "We were able to pin down the plane the Hollow resides in from a sample obtained in the course of the investigation. It's basically a vast endless sea. We are having less luck figuring out which creature is the Hollow—the Sumerians were less than descriptive in their texts, and we've been looking for hints in other histories without much luck.

"We know the same creature is responsible for all the deaths so far based on the magical signature found at the scene of the crimes, although the lack of a signature on the bodies suggests that it is not killing with magic per se, but a natural ability to suck souls out through the reflection of the victim's own eyes—windows to the soul and all that. That seems to fit with an account from the lone survivor of an attack.

"The best theory we could come up with is that this thing is simply hungry and it eats souls. Ancient Sumer effectively dried up its watering hole when they destroyed their mirrors and took precautions around still water, and it left to find another place to hunt. Unfortunately, Janice drew its attention back to the mortal realm and we are back on the menu. We had hoped that getting rid of the ritual focus object would alleviate the situation, but it has not." Everyone knew how serious it was when the twins didn't know what was going on and when Dot let Chloe talk so long without making any acerbic remarks.

"As you can see," Martinez picked up the baton, "things are escalating quickly. Fortunately, we are still in the early days, thanks to Keller's tip. It isn't too late to put a pin in this, if we can figure out just how to do that." Martinez finished her introduction with a positive spin and opened the floor to questions and ideas.

"Any luck on figuring out how Keller was able to even contact this outer plane? It's not exactly common knowledge, and maybe that could give us a clue on how to shut it down," Moncrief suggested.

"A check of her financials don't show any recent large withdrawals, transfers, or purchases. She purchased the mirror she'd used in the ritual online through a credible auction house, and besides her sustaining memberships to a handful of organizations, she made no recent large donations. I did a thorough search of her house yesterday afternoon and didn't find any ancient scrolls or long-lost codices. On her computer, she had a hi-res digital copy of the Voynich manuscript, but what are the chances she decoded that and didn't write it down somewhere?" Martinez responded, waving her hands.

"So this thing has the ability to contact the mortal realm without actually entering it?" Hobgoblin asked.

"That's our understanding. If it was actually physically summoned here, I'm pretty sure we would all be dead," Dot replied. Martinez wasn't the only one who thought it must be dire if Dot was being serious.

"Is it possible for *us* to make contact with *its* realm?" Liu inquired with a calculating look in her eye.

"Possibly," Chloe answered. "What do you have in mind?"

"If someone was able to hurt it while it was feeding, why can't we bait it and kill it?" Liu theorized. Martinez could only imagine duck decoys, call whistles, and Elmer Fudd whispering, "Shhh. Be vewy vewy quiet. I'm hunting outsiders…" She stifled a laugh, *Man, I need to get some sleep.*

A round of head tilts and nods circled the table. "Anyone have any ideas how to kill it? Banishment bullets aren't going to do any good—it's already dining from home," Martinez noted.

"And getting shanked by an astral dagger is a far cry from killing it," Moncrief added with authority.

"Nuke it from orbit, it's the only way to be sure," Hobgoblin paraphrased *Aliens*. "If you can make a connection, we can deliver a bomb. They tend to kill everything, and even if ours doesn't, it should be enough to scare it away—convince it to return to where it has been feeding for the past couple of millennia. More cooperative prey, if you get my drift."

"I'm all for not being eaten, but wouldn't throwing explosives into the void be extraordinarily dangerous and reckless?" Liu asked.

"And what about the energy wave? We would have no way to control where and how the collateral damage went," Martinez added.

Hobgoblin shrugged. "If we put it on a timed denotation and closed the connection before it blew, we wouldn't be close to it. How many planes are between us and it? They'd absorb any residual energy."

Everyone was preoccupied with their own thoughts when Martinez finally spoke. "As much as I hate to say it, it's not a bad idea. But all this is contingent on connecting to an outer plane and passing an object through that connection. How the hell is that going to happen? Liu and I had to go to the Magh Meall just to send the mirror into the astral plane."

Weber cleared his throat. "In theory, I could coat a mirror with the astral shavings I already have. It wouldn't be a very big mirror, but it would allow the package to pass through it."

"Like electroplating on an atomic level?" Martinez ventured.

Weber's blue eyes lit up; Lancer hadn't failed to impress him yet. "Something like that," he replied, "but magically, of course."

"Okay, that would mean we could theoretically send 'the package' from the mortal realm," she adopted Weber's euphemism. "But that doesn't answer how we are going to establish a connection to the outer plane. I can't find any trace of Keller's ritual, and we couldn't scry it out of any of her divination objects. We might know which plane is it, but not how to reach it."

"And only crazy people go looking for outsiders," Dot added wryly. Martinez bobbed her head to concede to her point; she was glad to see the dour blonde back in sarcastic form. "Which is why I'll have to do it." A wave of puzzled looks rippled to Dot, and the only ones that seemed to follow her train of thought were her sister and Leader.

"Dot, you can't be serious," Chloe replied.

"You heard Martinez. If we don't act, we'll all be outsider fish food," she rebutted.

"You don't know that. There are a lot more people around now; maybe it will get full and fall back asleep," Chloe desperately grasped at straws.

"Dot," Leader spoke for the first time since the meeting began. "I'm not asking you to do this, but if you are willing to, I'll allow it." The electricity of her words sliced through the mounting tension between the sisters. Chloe backed down; this was Dot's decision.

Dot turned her blue eyes first to Leader and then to her sister. "I'll do it," she said resolutely.

"I'm sorry, but what exactly is Dot going to do?" Moncrief finally gave voice to all the bewildered at the table.

Dot addressed them all. "I'm going to mind meld with the Hollow and use that to make a connection to its native plane."

"Wait, like a Vulcan mind meld?" Martinez asked incredulously.

"Not exactly. That involves merging two minds into one through telepathy. I just need to zero in on its location, not understand it on a deeper level. I can use the nub of its… appendage…" Dot searched for the right anatomical term.

"I thought contact with outsiders was generally a bad idea and could evoke instant madness," Liu pointed out as delicately as possible.

"A notion popularized by Lovecraft," Dot said dismissively. "Not untrue, but perhaps a little exaggerated for dramatic effect."

"But it is a risk," Chloe clarified.

"And I'm not your typical person," Dot continued. "Chloe and I are two minds in one body. I'll get in, make the connection long enough for someone to deliver Hobgoblin's package, and then disconnect."

"Dot, there's got to be a better way than to risk losing your mind," Martinez reasoned.

"If there was, we'd be trying that instead of sitting in a situation room and taking suggestions from Hobgoblin," Dot snidely remarked. "No offense, pretty boy." She nodded to him.

"None taken," he answered with a charming grin.

"Dot, are you sure?" Chloe asked again.

In an uncharacteristic moment of tenderness, Dot reached for her sister's hand under the table and squeezed. "You'll pull me back. You always do."

"We have a lot of work to do and the sooner we shut this down, the better," Leader said, assuming control of the meeting. "Weber, get started on the mirror. Chloe and Dot, ready yourselves however you need. Hobgoblin, you're on the bomb—work with Weber on the size restrictions. I want the smallest profile for the biggest bang and remember, it's got to work underwater. Clover, see if you have anything at home that could assist in this endeavor. Lancer, find a safe place to do this. Aurora, I want you on defense—once the threshold between the worlds is open, anything can come through. Do whatever you have to do to make this happen; we'll cover the karmic debt. Just get it done."

Chapter Twenty

The van drove into the University District and wound through the rows of mowed lawns with clean edges. Liu was at the wheel with Hobgoblin riding shotgun. The twins sat in the middle bench seat with Moncrief in the back, keeping an eye on their equipment. It wasn't every day you transported magical artifacts with explosives and mirrors all in the same hold, which was why Hobgoblin wasn't allowed to drive. This was not the day to speed or take any more risks than necessary.

Liu pulled alongside the black Hellcat parked in front of the Tudor-style home. Martinez saw their approach in her rearview mirror and climbed out of the driver's seat with her field kit. She opened the gate to the backyard and unlocked the back door to the house to make unloading as discreet, smooth, and fast as possible. Coming up with the right location on such short notice was challenging, and while it was less than ideal, Keller's house ticked all the boxes. It was an unoccupied, private space the Hollow had been before that was already set up for casting, even if it was woefully lacking in chairs. Another place, one more magically secure, would only make the mission harder to execute since it relied on Dot making a connection to the outer planes; good security was designed to prevent such affairs.

Hobgoblin hopped out of the car and opened the sliding door for the twins. Liu joined him while Moncrief carefully handed the sensitive pieces of gear one at a time. Only after everything was unloaded did Moncrief climb out of the back with her personal bag—she never left home without it.

Hobgoblin whistled appraisingly as he passed the muscle car. "I've misjudged you, Martinez," he intonated as he passed her on his way into Keller's house.

"I haven't," she quipped. "Maybe if you showed up at the office more often, you'd know these things."

"And ruin his tan? Don't you know pretty boys wilt underground, Martinez," Dot joked. The gentle ribbing helped undercut the rising pressure.

They made their way to the house. "Oh my," Moncrief gasped upon entry.

"This is a lot to take in," Liu agreed as she did a visual sweep.

"To be fair to the deceased, I tossed it pretty good yesterday afternoon, so the mess is mine. But the décor, if that's what you want to call it, is all hers," Martinez qualified.

"Janice always had her own distinct aesthetic," Chloe diplomatically explained.

"Just wait until you see upstairs," Martinez foreshadowed

as she locked the door behind them and led them up the stairs to Keller's magic room. She opened the door and flicked on the light, stepping in to make way for the caravan behind her.

"It's very…cozy," Moncrief tapered off in an attempt to be positive.

Chloe put her index finger to her lips. "You know what this room needs?"

"A black light and lava lamp?" Martinez guessed.

"A hookah?" Liu took a stab.

"A harem to go with all these rugs and silk scarves?" Hobgoblin joined in as he placed Moncrief's heavy box beside the slate table.

"I was thinking a cleansing by fire," Dot conjectured.

"Some light," Chloe emphatically answered her own question, drawing up the shades a few inches to let in more light without compromising privacy. "There, now we can see what the hell we are doing."

Chloe and Dot pushed two chairs together, took a seat at the table, and prepared for the ritual sacrifice to Janus—who else would you petition but the god of doorways? Chloe cleaned the slate top, dried it, and meticulously chalked the protective circles, ensuring each symbol was correctly formed and touched the central circle just so. Dot set up the brazier and the ritual offerings: incense and strues with honey. A slightly sweet woody smell filled the room as she opened the Tupperware container filled with cakes; she slapped Hobgoblin's hand away as he reached for one. "These are for Janus. You can have one after the ritual if we are still alive," she chided him.

Hobgoblin sat beside Dot and unpacked Weber's mirror: a small circular piece a mere four inches in diameter. Opening the velvet pouch, he confirmed the glass was intact before placing it in the circle. Then he pulled out his package: a three-foot-long tube packed with C4 that was only three inches in diameter with two timed detonators strapped along its length.

"You should consult a doctor if it's been longer than four hours," Martinez sarcastically parroted the medical warnings. Even his bombs were phallic.

"Leader asked for the biggest payload with the smallest profile, and I always give a lady what she asks for," he professed casually.

"Boys and their toys," Moncrief observed as she took the final seat at the table between Hobgoblin and Chloe. Moncrief opened the large box and unearthed a mass of bubble wrap and quilts. She gingerly unwrapped the layers of protective cushion until she uncovered an old ceramic pot with a knob pitched into the top.

"Like you're one to talk—you brought a Parthian Battery," he called out the heiress; if anyone loved her toys, it was Moncrief, magical and otherwise.

"Wait, they're magic?" Martinez queried.

"Well, maybe not all of them but this one is," Moncrief averred. "Figured we could use it to boost the signal."

"Did you disable the smoke detectors?" Dot asked Martinez before lighting the charcoal.

"With all the smudging she did up here, it should be fine, but I took the batteries out of the one on the landing just to be safe," Martinez confirmed as she cleared the packing away from the table.

Liu positioned herself between the table and the door. In total, she had a dozen blades on her person, and if she didn't have to worry about concealment, they were a split second away from deployment. She methodically checked each knife one more time for chips or imperfections in either the blade or the magical sigils etched in silver, even though she knew she would find none. Providing defense for the ritual, she would not be using her will to power it and would instead be ready to attack—physically and magically—anything that might come through the mirror.

"You need anything?" Martinez asked her.

"Nope, I'm good," Liu replied as she strapped the full bandolier across her torso.

As the only person with the legal right to be in the house, Martinez was outside the circle as well, here to assist but staying free should someone come knocking on the door. She loaded her magazine with banishment bullets with the sigils etched in Sumerian, just in case.

Dot donned a pure white linen robe and her freshly washed and braided hair smelled of laurel and sage—this was close as she was going to get to a vestal virgin. The charcoal smoldered as Dot pulled out the mason jar containing the slimy nub. "Are we ready?"

No one voiced objection, and Dot began her litany. Martinez never would have guessed how sweet a voice Dot had as her lyric soprano soared over the smoke, made fragrant once Dot placed the incense over the coals. Those fluent in classical Latin could follow her verse, while everyone else—that being Hobgoblin and Martinez—simply followed the crests and falls of the cadence. Everyone at the table focused on powering Dot's ritual, weaving their will into her magic. Dot crumbled a cake and dolloped honey over it. The smoke sweetened as the sugar burned off.

Once Dot had finished extolling all the virtues of the two-headed god, she began her supplications. She unscrewed the mason jar, releasing the ripe smell of the decaying flesh. She poured it onto the fire, cleansing it and making it pure for Janus's inspection and intercession.

Dot closed her eyes and immediately the void loomed before her. She dangled herself just over its edge, holding tight to Chloe, who was firmly grounded in the mortal realm. She felt something approach from below: something big, something old, something curious. *Just a little bit closer*, Dot told herself in the worst game of chicken ever. She felt an inky tendril reach up and touch her outstretched finger.

Dot's eyes shot open and her speech became rapid and

incomprehensible, no longer the classical Latin of before. It was something that not even her sister could understand. Martinez reflexively drew her Glock. "Now!" Chloe yelled to Hobgoblin.

He set the first detonator to one minute and the second to ninety seconds—enough time to feed the tube through the mirror and close the connection, but not long enough for the Hollow to figure out what it was and try to spit it back out at them. He fed the pipe into the mirror with haste. "Done, break the connection!"

Chloe closed her eyes. "*Dot, it's time to go.*"

Dot's mind was so full of new things; she could learn so much more if only she stayed. "*Just a little longer, Chloe.*"

Liu watched intently as Chloe closed her eyes and Dot continued to spew her nonsensical stream of consciousness. A black tendril crept out of the mirror. The blade in her right hand flew and pinned it to the table. "It's trying to come through. Shut it down!"

Chloe heard Liu with one ear even though she was in a place that existed just between her and her twin. She summoned all her will and unleashed it. "*Dot—now!*" She pulled hard on her sister's hand and yanked her back from the precipice.

Dot fell silent and came to her senses and immediate looked to her sister. Chloe had beads of sweat rolling down her face and a worried look in her eyes. "Dot? Is it you?"

Dot blinked a few times and smugly grinned. "I told you you'd bring me back."

"You are such a pain!" Chloe yelled as she embraced her. For once, Dot let her.

Liu had grabbed another knife and Martinez still had her gun drawn. Hobgoblin kept his eye on his watch that was counting down. "How do we know if it went off?" Moncrief nervously filled the silence.

"Five, four, three, two—" Hobgoblin chanted but the sound of glass breaking interrupted his countdown. They looked at Weber's mirror, fractured like a spider's web from the other side but seemingly intact on theirs. "Well, that's not disturbing," he dryly remarked.

"Keller's mirror had magic residue on it too, and that was completely shattered. Let's get this back to the Mine where it will be safe," Martinez suggested, putting the mirror back into its velvet bag.

While everyone was packing up their gear, Hobgoblin picked up one of the cakes and took a hardy bite. He almost spit it out but when Martinez, Chloe, and Dot glared at him to reconsider, he managed to choke it down. "These are disgusting."

"They're baked on a bed of bay leaves and hardly have any sugar in them," Chloe clued him in.

"Then why did you let me eat it?" he asked indignantly.

Liu smiled. "It's like letting your kid eat baker's chocolate—if you don't, they'll never learn."

Chapter Twenty-One

Detroit, Michigan, USA
9th of August, 10:24 p.m. (GMT-4)

Terrible things happened everyday all over the world. If he thought too long on it, it would have depressed him, stirring his empathy and sense of justice, but that wasn't his job. Emmitt was there to find patterns and wade through the tragedies for connections, coincidences, and improbabilities.

Not all of them garnered mainstream media coverage; the more prestigious or sensational got their fifteen minutes of fame splashed in newsfeeds, shared on social media, or streamed at the bottom of the screen on a twenty-four-hour news station. There were other ways of finding things out, if you knew the back ways. How many unofficial reporters walked around with their tiny cameras amongst the billions all across the globe?

Sometimes he got lucky and was given prompts: find a connection between these three things, deep dig into person X, or look for more things that fit pattern Y. Those were the equivalent of scavenger hunts: he had a list and he just had to collect things and tick the boxes. Otherwise, he drifted through an endless sea of information.

His official title was Data Analyst at Discretion Minerals, boring enough to dissuade most from asking more about his work. The droll would make some joke about it being monotonous while the polite would say something paradoxical, like "oh, how interesting!" before changing subjects. Those that expressed genuine curiosity would get a surprised and terse explanation, "I mine big data for statistical relevance," but nothing more could be said. Those were the rules.

Emmitt stared at his three screens, each monitoring different events at different locations. While it was connected to the larger world, it was separate from the intranet employed at the Salt Mine. No communication was the only way to keep the system secure. Everything had to be typed out or physically transferred.

He had been halfway through his shift when something caught his eye: a report of twenty-five dead at a dance conservatory in France. Those practicing inside had asphyxiated, and the building had been cleared for fear it was a gas leak. It could be nothing, but that wasn't Emmitt's job to decide. It fit the pattern, and he'd flagged it for further consideration before combing the web for more.

That's when he found the video: someone had been streaming live at a club in Moscow. Emmitt checked the timestamp and did the time zone math—it happened four hours ago. He saved the video, scanned it, and transferred it onto a USB flash drive, where it would be scanned again before being input into the Salt Mine's intranet—there was a protocol to these things. Emmitt sent a message to Lancer and Leader before turning his attention to his three screens. It never stopped, neither the misery nor the news.

*****

Leader watched the video again. The camera was front facing, capturing a group having a night on the town. She muted it, having no desire to listen to their narration shouted over the loud music again, and focused on the background. She could just make out the activity behind them but the scope became clearer once the person filming the video of the group caught a glimpse of their own reflection and moved forward, revealing the swath of people behind them drawn off the dance floor to the periphery lined with mirrors. They reached out and touched the mirrors, and when one fell, another came to take their place at the glass.

Normally, she would send an agent to confirm—there was no way to be absolutely certain it was the Hollow without salting—but this was far from a routine situation. First, it was in Moscow, solidly Ivory Tower territory; it wasn't off-limits, but there was a certain level of caution and tact required. Second, it would take far too much time. If the Hollow behind either or both of the European attacks, it would appear Hobgoblin's bomb did little more than make it hungrier and that the deaths had escalated from single attacks to mass feedings. However, there had been no more killings in Detroit since the intervention. Knowing Hobgoblin, his solution to the dispersal of targets would be a bigger bomb.

Leader leaned back and took comfort in Jan Brueghel the Elder's *The Temptation of Saint Anthony*. While Saint Anthony wandered the Egyptian desert, he was beset by demons that he resisted and rejected. Besides the evocative use of form, contrast, and composition, it was a good reminder on how to conduct one's self when dealing with fiends. She looked one more time at the questions scribbled on her notepad, all but one scratched out for one reason or another. Most often, they were too vague or open to interpretation—never advisable when making deals with a devil.

She only had so many questions left after all these years; she was parsimonious with the resource because it was finite, and she really didn't want to try to capture Furfur a second time for more. A ravenous outsider with a known history of nearly wiping out humanity once before seemed an appropriate level of threat. To ask another of similar age and knowledge as Furfur would cost dearly and come with some uncertainly—at least Furfur was caged and bound.

She left her office on the fourth floor and summoned the elevator with her palm. Once inside, she held her eye and hand to the scanners and pressed level six. The crystalline walls sparkled as she passed through the long corridors, beyond the stacks and the empty central desk to another elevator, this one with twelve stops.

Leader pressed the button for the twelfth floor, the lowest level of the Salt Mine, and composed herself on the ride down another four hundred feet into the earth. There was an art to extracting the most useful information in the fewest possible questions. Without knowing the answer, she had to find the question that led to what she really needed to know. It was like chess with more pieces and less rules, and it required more than just intelligence to play. Clarity of purpose and discipline were paramount to avoid distraction and ignore baiting, and an agile mind was necessary to compensate for the Great Earl of Hell's obfuscation. After all, he was only bound to respond honestly, not to be helpful in his answer.

When the elevator finally stopped, the doors opened to another hallway, this one leading to a forty-foot square single room. The music from a console game echoed down the saline chamber and crescendoed as Leader stepped into the room. "Hello, Furfur," she announced her presence to the large man parked on the worn puce-colored couch. He was dressed in jeans and a black t-shirt, but kept a pair of short horns to hail to his linage. He paused his game and the music instantly cut out.

"Leader. To what do I owe this rare honor? Don't tell me you missed me," he greeted her coyly. She felt his will press against hers and rebuffed it.

"I have a question to ask you," she stated plainly.

He rose from his upholstered throne, standing well over a foot taller than the petite woman. She was undaunted. "A question?" he asked, bemused. "Enumerated and precious. Things must be bad," he attempted to goad her, but saw it was to no avail. "You take all the fun out of our tête-à-têtes," Furfur complained. "A devil could die of boredom in here. Very well, ask your question."

Leader recited the carefully crafted question written upstairs on her notepad, "How do we destroy the outsider known amongst the ancient Sumerians as the Hollow?"

"Oh, not just a question, but a *serious* question." He giggled before answering honestly, "You don't. It is immense and endless." A foul grin slid across his face. "Have you another question?"

"Yes," Leader replied, much to Furfur's surprise. "If we can't kill it, how do we hide all the mortals from the Hollow without destroying or covering all the mirrors?"

A flicker of recognition passed across his countenance as he recognized the care taken when crafting her question. Leader's gray hawkish eyes did not flinch. "You've always been a canny one," he almost complimented her.

"An honest reply will do, Furfur," she cut his banter short.

"Seek he who found his reward and punishment in his reflection." Armed with his answer, Leader turned to leave. "That's two questions less. I do hope this creature doesn't feast on your soul before I get the chance to," he taunted her. She remained unmoved.

After a moment, the sound of his game came back on, as if the threat had just been conversation about the weather, which was Leader's cue to trip the fuse on the nearby power box on the wall. The TV and console went dead. A stream of obscenities descended upon her and she felt the heat of his rage as she walked down the passage and left the Great Earl of Hell to stew in his impertinence.

Back in the elevator, she pressed level seven instead of returning to the library's floor. Leader had widgets to position and schemes to put in motion before she could breathe a sigh of relief.

Chapter Twenty-Two

Detroit, Michigan, USA
10th of August, 4:30 p.m. (GMT-4)

Martinez followed the signs to long-term parking; she found it ironic that she had to park with the plebs despite the fact that she was catching a ride on a private plane, but that's what she got for not having a chauffer to drop her off directly on the tarmac. Her disassembled Glock with an array of magical bullets was packed in the secret compartment of her luggage out of habit, even though she wouldn't be going through security. She roamed a section of the Detroit Metro Airport completely new to her until she found herself on the stretch of runway reserved for private charters. The jets gleamed in the late afternoon sun, and Martinez peered through her sunglasses, looking for the G650 in metallic cobalt with a silver stripe—Clover's plane.

The wheels of her suitcase rhythmically clicked against the textured asphalt as she approached the jet. It was closed up, and Martinez wasn't sure what the protocol was. Did one knock or wave down the pilot? Was it impolite to bang on the side? Did one have to ask permission to board like with ships? Martinez pulled out her phone and texted Moncrief instead. Within a minute, the door opened and a staircase lowered. "Good afternoon, Ms. Martinez," a uniformed steward greeted her. "May I help you with your luggage?"

Martinez kept her grip. "No, I'll be fine. Thank you."

"As you wish," he acquiesced with a slight bow. "Ms. Moncrief is waiting for you inside. We should be taking off shortly. Let me know if you require anything to settle."

Martinez proceeded up the stairs. "Thank you…"

"Jeffery," he answered her implicit question.

"Thank you, Jeffery," Martinez annunciated his name.

"Oh good, you're here!" Moncrief cooed at Martinez's appearance through the jet's entryway as if she hadn't just received her text. She looked right out of a 1960's movie; her blonde hair streaked with sunshine was divided in high pigtails with a prominent bump at the crown, her fitted short-sleeved polo shirt flared at the hips of her slim black capris, and she wore ballet flats. All she needed was a clutch, a boxy double-breasted jacket, and scarf around her hair and she could have been an extra for *Breakfast at Tiffany's*. "I was getting worried."

"A weekend in Greece? I wouldn't miss it for the world," Martinez quipped as she took it all in. The front section seated four in plushy leather captain chairs that reclined and laid flat for overnight travel. The next section looked more like a living room, with a long bank seat opposite a flat-screen television. Martinez couldn't see beyond the next partition and stopped herself from craning her neck out of curiosity.

Moncrief smiled at her guest's reserved manner. "Let's get you settled and I can give you the tour before takeoff."

"Where should I put this?" Martinez indicated the luggage she dragged behind her.

"Jeffery didn't take care of that?" Moncrief puzzled.

"He offered but I declined," Martinez explained.

A spark of recognition glinted in her bright eyes. "Jeffery, can you show Teresa where she can stow her luggage?"

"Yes, Miss," he humbly replied.

Martinez followed the steward through the living room, which had a mini fridge and a fully stocked bar, through a dining room with a kitchenette, to a bedroom with a full bath and closet. "There should be room in here with Ms. Moncrief's luggage."

Martinez stared at the tower of cases expertly packed like a Jenga tower. "That's all Alicia's?"

"Miss does prefer to be prepared for all potentialities," he stated neutrally.

Martinez slid her suitcase into a nook and kept hold of her shoulder bag which contained the mission information. She wasn't sure how much Moncrief had been briefed, but they had hours in the air for her to familiarize herself with it. The heiress was her only on-site backup and in Martinez's book, forewarned was forearmed.

Moncrief was lounging in the living room when Martinez returned with Jeffery in tow. "All settled? Good! How about something to drink?"

Martinez took a seat on the remarkably plump cabin chair opposite Moncrief. "I'll be fine with water," she answered.

Moncrief squinted her eyes in thought. "I'll have a blood orange mimosa," she placed her order. Jeffery got to work. "Have you been to Greece before?" She turned to Martinez. "You'll just love it! Even though this isn't the best time to visit, unless you like the heat."

Martinez politely nodded as Moncrief filled in both sides of the conversation with ease. She hadn't worked much with Clover, and what she knew about her was largely by reputation. Moncrief was generally well received by the other agents, not just because of her bountiful resources but because there was an effortlessness about her, a resolute confidence that came with money and breeding. She watched the animated young woman chatter and wondered what was behind the smile and dimples, the witty banter, and the designer clothes.

Jeffery presented them their beverages on a platter before excusing himself, closing the doors and giving them some privacy. Moncrief stopped mid-sentence about how beautiful Santorini was this time of year and her face dropped the lightness behind her smile. "So, why are we going into the Magh Meall in Greece, and why did I need to free up a million dollars on short notice?"

Martinez choked on her water. "I'm sorry, did you say 'a million'?"

"That's what Leader said over the phone," Moncrief replied.

"And that's all she gave you?" Martinez marveled. "I thought my briefings were thin."

Moncrief laughed. "Leader tells us what we need to do our jobs. My job is to be rich, well-connected, and magically endowed."

"Well, I'm going to need a little more than that from you," Martinez responded honestly.

Moncrief's smile turned mischievous. "Good. I'm more than a pretty face with a private jet."

Martinez pulled out a green folder with AGENT RESTRICTED – SM EYES ONLY in red lettering. "I'll show you mine if you show me yours?"

Moncrief narrowed her eyes. "What makes you think I have anything special?"

"You're Clover—you have all the goodies," Martinez answered.

Moncrief tossed her head back with a full-throated guffaw. "Is that what the other agents say about me?"

Martinez smiled. "I was also advised that you would 'take care' of the other necessary gear." Martinez bobbed her head side-to-side. "To be fair, you can't expect me to believe you brought all that luggage without packing something serious when you know we're going into the Magh Meall. Greek fae are notoriously hardcore."

"Ugh," Moncrief groaned. "You have no idea. Fae are

pompous and tedious at the best of times, but they are even worse after mingling with deities."

A smooth voice came over the intercom, advising all on board to ready for takeoff. Jeffery knocked before re-entering the lounge and retrieving Moncrief's empty glass. Martinez secured her possessions and buckled in.

*****

"So you always travel like this?" Martinez questioned in disbelief. "No taking off your shoes, no limit on carry-on liquids, no full body scans or pat downs?"

Moncrief wrinkled her nose. "Oh God no! What would be the point of having a private jet and flying commercial?" She sipped her dry burgundy to wash the distasteful notion out of her mind. A silent pair of hands cleared the remains of dinner from the table and presented a platter of fruit and cheese. Martinez swirled her glass of wine and breathed deeply before imbibing—she could get used to traveling in style.

"So what do you think?" Martinez queried Moncrief as soon as the staff left them alone.

"If anyone else had cooked up this scheme, I would have called them insane," Moncrief concluded after some thought. "But Leader is rarely wrong."

"Rarely?" Martinez poked at the qualifier.

"Personal motto: Never say never," Moncrief pontificated.

"There are more things in heaven and earth, Horatio, than are dreamt of in your philosophy," she quoted Hamlet.

"I'm still processing that Narcissus was real," Martinez admitted.

"A beautiful but egotistical man that was part fae, roaming the mortal realm in the zenith of Greek divine power, being aptly punished for his cruel vanity?" Moncrief postulated rhetorically. "It tracks. Greek deities are remarkably human in their pettiness and I'm like a three amongst the fae—they do like pretty things."

"All that glitters is not gold," Martinez recited the aphorism reflexively.

"If you bust out in 'Stairway to Heaven,' I'm tossing you out of the plane," Moncrief warned her.

Martinez pshawed. "Do I look like Hobgoblin?"

Moncrief giggled as she finished her wine. "Come on, I'll show you what I brought, and then we can catch some shut eye before we land."

Martinez had just enough wine to feel giddy at the prospect of getting a peek inside Moncrief's tower of luggage. She sat expectantly on the edge of the bed, like a kid under the Christmas tree while Moncrief pulled out the bags she had packed herself. "We don't have an appointment with the fae, but I brought appropriate dress for both of us just in case we run into them," she spoke while she unpacked two sets of beige clothing.

Martinez fingered the linen cuff as she held hers up against her body to check the fit. "So that's why they measured me during onboarding."

"I have a summer and winter set for each agent, just in case," Moncrief explained. "Absolutely no metal in or on it, and it should be quite cool and breathable. I'm assuming you packed your gun, which you can bring, but it's more socially acceptable to arm yourself with enchanted weapons—the fae are a little behind the times in terms of technology," Moncrief said as an aside.

"I can sort of understand. If you are one of the fae and can already accomplish the same thing with magic, do you really need technology?"

"Well, magic can be wonky and temperamental," Moncrief countered.

"So can technology," Martinez drily pointed out. "We're all one shitty software update from bricking our phones. Talk about inciting a panic." She got back on track when she saw a gleaming pair of karambits with silver runes inlayed along their curved blades.

"I packed these for you to use. They are cold iron and enchanted to be particularly irritating to most supernatural creatures—think fire ant bite meets jellyfish sting. I figured you've probably had more training with hand-to-hand fighting and knife-skills than swords," Moncrief guessed.

"If I'm using these instead of my gun, we're in trouble,"

Martinez speculated as she picked up the knives and appraised their balance. "Still, better safe than sorry."

"I know a fantastic weapons trainer if you're interested. Choreographing fight scenes in movies and training actors to look the part pays the bills, but he's a serious boss with all manner of melee weapons," Moncrief offered.

"Let's see how things go in the Magh Meall and with the Hollow before I go making future plans," Martinez gave a non-committal maybe. "You got anything else in there?"

"Everything we need to enter, some culturally appropriate gifts that aren't magical, my weapon," Moncrief rattled off her mental list of the contents in the unopened baggage. "I was told it was an acquisition mission and if we encountered anyone, it was largely going to be diplomatic in nature," she prefaced, but the playful glint in her eyes belied more to come. "But, just in case this thing turns into a smash and grab, I brought these."

Moncrief pulled out two obsidian rings polished to a gleam and placed one in Martinez's hand; the cold stone was smooth to her touch. "These are return rings—if you find yourself traveling outside of the mortal realm and you need to get out fast, you think the activation phrase and poof!—you're back."

"Is it safe to put on?" Martinez asked before indulging her curiosity.

"Sure," Moncrief confirmed as she repacked the weapons and clothing neatly—linen wrinkled so easily.

Martinez gasped with delight as it resized itself for her

finger—it was her first magic ring. "Do they all do that?"

"Generally, although technically it doesn't have to," she answered thoughtfully. "It seems rather silly not to make it self-sizing, especially since magic generally longs to be used."

"Why do you have two?" Martinez inquired.

"They were my parents'; they went everywhere together," Moncrief responded with a wistful smile that left as quickly as it came. "A word of caution—don't use this as a shortcut home. It's much safer to return to the circle, because you know where you will end up in the mortal realm. This is strictly for emergencies and if you have to use it, hope that you don't appear over a cliff or in the depths of the sea. Geography sort of tracks from here to the Magh Meall, but it isn't an exact science—wonky and temperamental, remember?"

Martinez nodded, slid the ring off her finger, and handed it back to Moncrief for safekeeping. "So we're really going to do this?"

"What's the body count up to?" Moncrief asked.

"Nearly a thousand suspected in mass events across the globe since we set off the bomb, but I'm guessing the actual count is higher once you factor in less public deaths, individuals, and attacks in remote areas with less news coverage," Martinez declared, tacitly answering her own question. "To Hobgoblin's credit, there have been no mass events in North America."

"Don't tell him that. It will only encourage him," Moncrief smirked. "Jeffery should have everything ready for you:

blankets, pillows, ear plugs, eye covers, whatever you need."

"Less risk of eminent death would be nice," Martinez joked as she rose from the bed.

"Think of the bragging rights you'll have after tomorrow," Moncrief tried to insert some levity.

"Dead men tell no tales," Martinez replied with a touch of gallows humor.

Moncrief stopped her packing and looked up at Martinez. "No one's died on my watch yet, and unlike you, *I'm* not planning to break any records tomorrow." Behind the glamorous facade was something hard as steel.

Martinez let it lie between them. "Good night, Alicia."

"Good night, Teresa."

Chapter Twenty-Three

Pullup Lake, MI, USA
10th of August, 8:30 p.m. (GMT-4)

Sukchu Yi sat upon his perch on the pier and watched the sun set, painting the sky in wondrous beauty before plunging below the horizon and leaving the water to be illuminated by the reflection of the seemingly brighter moon. He puffed away on his pipe, blowing smoke rings into the night. The melody of dusk was well underway: a lyric wail of a loon, the chittering of cicadas, and the hypnotic stridulation of grasshoppers en masse.

He had brought his fishing gear. The two hundred-acre lake was home to Northern Pike, Perch, and Bullheads, but he wasn't sure if anything was biting tonight. Luckily, catching fish wasn't always the point of fishing. Sukchu Yi attached his lure and fresh bait, ready to cast his line into the dark waters once night had officially fallen. He liked fishing at night, when there was less boat traffic on the water and fewer people to bother him and the fish.

A warm breeze blew over the water with just the hint of cooling; he breathed out smoky creations that soared with the wind. Despite the serene landscape, Yi was unsettled. Unlike other nearby lakes, Pullup was shallow and required strategically placed windmills to prevent freezing over the winter; it lacked the depth necessary for his foreboding trepidation. And yet, the angler had the niggling notion that something lurked beneath the surface, and he was certain the fish could perceive this turbulence—that was why he hadn't caught anything the past few days.

He heard a branch snap off in the distance—one hundred yards to the southeast. He kept his position steady and waited to hear the call of a friendly voice; the locals called him Chuck. When none came, Yi maintained his posture and closed his eyes, swirling his mind's eye out like a corkscrew. A smile crept upon his wrinkled face, bronzed by the long days of summer. "You might as well come out, Penny. You've already scared away the fish," he called as he pulled in his line.

A petite woman no more than 5'2" stepped out of the brush. Her hiking boots were secured over the cuff of her jeans and her arms covered; she held no truck with mosquitoes or ticks. She shook her salt-and-pepper hair in mild disbelief. "How *do* you do that?"

Yi chuckled. "You may be old, but I am older still." He pulled out two beers from his cooler before closing it and patting the top. "Take a seat."

She stepped forward with caution and accepted his invitation of hospitality. "I wasn't sure what kind of reception I would receive, considering how things went the last time we saw each other." She wiped down the bottle and popped the top.

"You were the one that shot first and asked questions later, remember?" he chided. His round face widened as he smiled, and his almond eyes narrowed even more. "Penny, what brings you to my neck of the woods? I'm an old fool, but not so much to think this is a social call."

She looked out at the water. "I need your help." She sipped her beer and waited for a response.

He puffed more fragrant smoke and answered, "My helping days are over."

"It isn't for me," she clarified. "It's something much bigger than that."

"It's always something bigger," he grumbled, throwing his arms in the air. "That's the problem—too many fires to put out when the world's aflame."

She sat tall on the cooler. "You'll forgive me if I don't sit back and watch it all burn."

Yi exploded in laughter. "I see the years have not made you any less proud or stubborn."

"You have no idea how far I can bend; I just choose not to," she replied, giving him a sideways glance. "Some practitioner drew the attention of an outsider that had been dormant since the days of Ancient Sumer, and all our previous attempts at containment have failed."

"And you have an idea?" he guessed.

"That is sort of my forte," she modestly commented.

Yi let his bowl cool before knocking out the spent leaves. "Pen, you are more than capable as a magician. Why do you need my help?"

She allowed herself a small grin at his almost-compliment. "Because what is required is on the fringe of my wheelhouse, but right up your alley."

That piqued Yi's interest. "What do you need?"

"I need a spell, something that will affect all the world's mirrors and reflective surfaces," she responded.

"That's some big magic," he conceded, but there was timbre in his voice. It had been a long while since he'd tried anything that substantial. "Hypothetically speaking, that magnitude of sympathetic magic would require some serious materials."

"I have an astral-coated mirror that has made contact with its home plane, and I have my people going into the Magh Meall for the waters of Narcissus," she laid out her cards.

He took a long drink of his beer. "That's one thing I've missed about you, Pen. You never go in half-assed."

"Will you do it?" she inquired earnestly.

"Yes," he eventually answered. "But only because the fish aren't biting and because it must be bad for you to ask a favor."

"I have another request," she admitted almost sheepishly. "My people don't call me by my name. To them, I'm simply Leader."

Yi loaded another bowl, this one for considering. "Don't worry about me, Penny. I won't give away your secret."

Chapter Twenty-Four

Mystras, Greece
11th of August, 10:40 a.m. (GMT+3)

"Are you sure this is the right place?" Martinez questioned as she scanned the forested side of the mountain. "I don't see any trace of standing water here."

Moncrief double-checked her GPS. "These are the coordinates Leader sent me," she said dubiously. "Maybe that's why we have to go to the Magh Meall—the topography in the mortal realm has shifted?"

While the myths generally agreed that Narcissus was a hunter, there was some dispute on where he was from and which mountains he prowled when Nemesis's retribution for brutally spurning Echo occurred. According to Leader, it was somewhere near Sparta and Mystras along the slopes of the Taygetos Mountains, a region dotted with small rivers and lakes. Unfortunately, the airfield in Sparta was for military use only; consequently, they'd had to land in Kalamata, which was just as close but required a more circuitous route. Moncrief, who'd received coordinates for their next port of call from Leader during the night, had left her staff with firm instructions: ready the plane for takeoff on their return in the late afternoon.

After a two-hour drive in their SUV loaded with supplies, they had gotten as close to the site as they could by car and made the rest of the trek by foot. Martinez wiped the beads of sweat from her brow; the climb up had been challenging with all their gear despite the coolness of the morning and altitude. She spied a clear patch of ground large enough to have a picnic and shrugged off the straps of her pack. "It's as good a place as any to enter. I'll get started on the circle if you set everything else up."

They worked in silence, alternatively blessed with a salty breeze from the sea or a hint of pine and cypress from the forest. From their location, they looked down upon the ancient ruins that loomed over modern Mystras. Martinez cut into the dry soil with ease, methodically forming a six-inch-deep trench. Moncrief laid out the picnic and the ritual accoutrements; she was an old hand at entering the middle lands. By the time Martinez completed the circle and put the shovel aside, Moncrief had everything in place and was checking her phone for a signal: four bars.

Martinez marveled at the spread—it was the picture of a picnic, down to the red-and-white checkered blanket. Quartered sandwiches containing a myriad of spreads were arranged on a tiered stand with choice sweets and cakes near the top. There was a basket of scones with clotted cream and strawberry jam, and miraculously, the Perrier and caviar were still chilled.

"Are you going to stare at it or eat it?" Moncrief teased, looking up from her phone.

"It's almost too pretty to eat," Martinez picked out an array of savories. She bit into the first sandwich: salmon mousse; the salty creaminess took her back to simpler times. They tucked in, eating and drinking their fill until it was time for their songs of supplication. They began their hour of meditation once Moncrief's small clock chimed noon and opened their eyes when it struck thirteen.

The air smelled clean and sweet, untouched by industrial pollution and exhaust. Martinez took in her surroundings among a thin stand of trees and questioned her travel partner. "Alicia, where are all the trees?"

Moncrief breathed deeply, taking in the Magh Meall before steadying her mind for the task ahead. "Sacred places are clearings, and we're in the ancient world now—throw a stone and you'll hit a place that was sacred to someone at some time."

Martinez did her own inventory before leaving the safety of the circle: return ring, amber periapt, rosary, enchanted karambits, gun loaded with banishment bullets, mirror, and waterskin. "Wait—there are fewer trees in the Magh Meall here? Where do all the visiting fae frolic?"

"Wherever they want," Moncrief retorted. "Not all faeries are quaint forest-dwelling darlings making pixie rings out of mushrooms. Think of these as urbane faeries."

"So how do we find Narcissus's pond?" Martinez adjusted

her stride to follow in step with the shorter blonde.

"Ask one of the locals. We should be in the neighborhood," she answered matter-of-factly. There was no trace of the cheerful frivolity Martinez had become accustomed to. She was no longer a jaunty heiress; she was Clover assisting Lancer. True to her word, once they cleared the tree line, they merged into a crowd of creatures composed of all different forms and colors. The emergence of two mortals from the forest garnered a wide array of reactions. While most went about their affairs with a few curious looks, others openly stared, unable to look away from the mortals' inherent ugliness.

Martinez would have liked to stay and creature watch, but she was acutely aware they were on a time-sensitive mission. Moncrief was busy cutting a path through the traffic with her inimitable presence; she might not be fae, but she could summon a sufficient amount of aplomb when necessary. Martinez shadowed her while keeping a close watch on her possessions.

They approached a stunning fae with thick luscious chestnut locks pinned up only to spill out over its bare tawny shoulders; a scant wrap sufficed as clothing. It could have passed for human were it not for the gossamer wings sprouting from its shoulder blades. "Excuse me, we are looking for the waters of Narcissus," Moncrief stated resolutely without a trace of question or request.

The fae beauty barely acknowledged Martinez, but deigned

to speak to Moncrief. "Follow the flowers and pay the giant," it answered brusquely.

Martinez waited until they were out of earshot. "The giant?"

Moncrief shrugged. "I hope it likes olive oil, cheese, and honey or this may be a short mission. We are not prepared to deal with an angry giant." She spotted a line of bi-colored flowers bearing six white petals and a golden central trumpet lining a foot-beaten path leading farther up into the forested mountains. "I think that's our yellow brick road."

The crowd thinned the further they ventured, and the pair traversed quietly. Eventually, they were the only two traveling on the path when they passed a cave mouth. "Who seeks entry to the waters of Narcissus?" a booming voice rumbled from within.

"Those who shun the weight of vanity," Moncrief replied reverently as she curtseyed.

A thoughtful hum vibrated the air in front of them. "And what have you brought for Aristaeus?"

"I honor the old ways," she responded as she unpacked the basket: an amphora of olive oil, a wheel of sheep's cheese, and a jar of honey.

An enormous hand five times larger than a man's emerged from the cave and claimed Moncrief's offerings. Aristaeus sniffed the air and turned his attention to Martinez. "And what have you brought?"

"She is with me," Moncrief cut in quickly. "My humble servant." Martinez bowed subserviently to sell her cover, but kept her head high enough to have adequate peripheral vision.

The giant took another short inhalation. "Your servant has something that smells good."

Moncrief shot Martinez a beseeching look. *What do you have?*

I have no idea! Martinez answered with her eyes as she opened her bag and frantically searched, finding a pound of beef jerky she had neglected to remove in her haste to get out of town.

Prostrate, Martinez offered Aristaeus her dried meats. "A paltry offering for one so great, but it is all that I have."

Adequately flattered by her words, the giant received her gift. "You may approach the waters. Be wary of what you find," he commanded by rote.

As they crested the hill, an entire meadow opened up below them covered with trumpets in every shade of yellow and orange, each ringed in white. Dots of honey, dijon, apricot, pumpkin, and amber shimmered in the bright purple sunlight, like thick daubs of paint in an impressionistic painting. At the end of the slope was a lake vast enough that the greenery on the other side was indistinct. "This is a pond?" Martinez whispered under her breath.

"Fae are so dramatic," Moncrief sighed and trod toward the lake. "What would the mortal realm look like if we did *this* every time someone was a vain ass to a shy person that liked them?" Martinez followed in her steps to avoid trampling as few blooms as necessary, even though every fiber of her body wanted to roll down the hill and breathe in their intoxicating bouquet. They demanded she experience them fully, but she focused on her mission and ignored them as best she could.

Once she reached the water's edge, she unscrewed the top of the waterskin and knelt down with her eyes closed and immersed the leather waterskin under the cool water. She listened for the slurping sounds to end—she didn't dare look at her reflection, considering how well that worked out for Narcissus—and once it was full, she hoisted the sack out of the lake and checked that the seared runes on its side faintly glowed blue. She dried the outside as much as possible, careful not to get any of the water near her mouth.

"We're all good," she called back to Moncrief, but when she looked up, the blonde was nowhere to be seen.

"Clover…where are you?" Martinez hollered and only heard giggles, but from no visible source. Martinez stepped away from the lake, sealed the top and stowed the waterskin in her bag, and pulled her rosary out of her pocket. *Hail Mary, full of grace…* She summoned her will and touched her return ring, focusing on its mate. Drawn up the hill by her spell, Martinez came to an abrupt halt—Moncrief should be right in front of her, but no one was there. Then she remembered Moncrief wielded Arthur's blade.

"Alicia, I give up!" Martinez yelled out, pretending to be at a loss. "You win. Olly olly oxen free!" She slipped her hand onto the hilt of one of her daggers just in case Moncrief wasn't herself—she was more likely to recover from a dagger wound than a bullet.

Moncrief blinked back into vision, crouched in the tall grass and colorful heads. She was holding Carnwennan loosely in one hand and stifling a giggle with the other. "I thought you'd never find me!" she giddily exclaimed. *Dear lord, she's as high as a kite!* Martinez beseeched any deity listening. "Now it's your turn to hide!" Moncrief declared.

"Hey, that's not fair. My weapon doesn't let me disappear," Martinez played along. "Why don't we play a different game? Race you back to the circle! Last one there is a rotten egg," she taunted.

"Oh, you're on!" Moncrief accepted the challenge. In one quick motion, she stood, sheathed her dagger in its red leather holster, and took off up the hill. Between her longer stride and her training, Martinez had no difficulty keeping up but stayed just behind Moncrief to make sure she was on track. They made good time, and Moncrief was doing a victory dance as she dashed in the circle first. "You're a rotten egg!"

Martinez took her licks with dignity, glad to be back in the safety of the circle. "You kicked my butt! You wanna take a selfie?"

Moncrief stopped mid-twirl. "Yes!" she exclaimed. There

was wild excitement in her wide eyes. "Best. Idea. Ever."

Martinez patted down her pockets. "I don't have my phone!"

"We can use mine," Moncrief added helpfully, running her thumbs over the surface to unlock it.

"I better take it—my arms are longer," Martinez pointed out.

Moncrief handed over her phone and started posing while Martinez tapped out the message with her thumb hovering over send. "Okay, ready?"

Martinez broke the circle with her will, and they were back among the forests of Taygetos. Martinez tapped send and held her breath—she had never given word to release one million dollars before and hoped it traveled faster than karma. She closed her eyes and waited for her fate; she was the one carrying something back from the Magh Meall.

"Teresa?" Moncrief mewed as she rolled on the checkered blanket. "Why does my head feel like I went on a tequila bender?"

Martinez opened her eyes and saw Moncrief sprawled amongst the remains of the picnic. *If this is death, at least it's well catered.* She popped another bottle of water and drank deeply before helping herself to a scone with plenty of cream and jam. "What do you remember?"

"We were going down the hill toward the water. I was waiting for you and smelling the flowers. Next thing I know, we're here," Moncrief puzzled.

Martinez handed her a bottle of water. "Next time, don't smell the flowers."

Moncrief chugged the whole thing. "Did we get it?"

Martinez patted her bag. "We got it."

"And the money's sent?" she asked before inhaling two sandwich quarters at the same time.

Martinez handed back her phone. "Yup."

Moncrief paused her gluttony and abashedly apologized, "I'm so sorry I lost it back there."

Martinez recalled the allure of rolling down the hill with abandon and shrugged. "Wonky and temperamental."

"Thanks for getting me out of there," Moncrief spoke with deliberate gratitude, pondering how long she would have lasted in that state of mind before eating or drinking something in the Magh Meall.

"I'm not sure I could have found you without these," Martinez confessed, tapping the return ring on her middle finger. "Tell you what, you can make it up to me with a proper girls' weekend in Greece."

"Deal," Moncrief immediately agreed.

"Now, I have a delivery to make," Martinez declared as she started packing up everything. Moncrief staggered to her feet and Martinez gave her the lighter bag. "And I'm driving."

Chapter Twenty-Five

Pullup Lake, MI, USA
12th of August, 8:00 p.m. (GMT-4)

Martinez followed the GPS on her phone down another dirt road: her destination was five hundred yards ahead. She could see why Georgie liked it up here—plenty of quiet nature to drown out all the calculated order and chaos of the modern world. Throw in a spouse, a couple of kids, a dog, maybe a camper, and it was almost a Norman Rockwall scene. Little did the Yoopers know they had a serious shaman amongst them that went by the name of Chuck.

She cut the engine and pulled out her bag and a flashlight; it was still light out, but she would need it for the walk back from the lake in the dark. As anticipated, a lone figure sat on the pier. "You Chuck?" she hollered.

"Might be," a pensive voice called back. "Depends on what you want."

"I'm here to see a man about a mirror," Martinez spoke in code.

A ring of smoke floated over his head. "Then I'm your man."

She approached Sukchu Yi, dressed in ceremonial robes

instead of his fishing gear. "Have any problems finding the place?" he made polite conversation.

"Nope, but getting these was a different story," she answered honestly, patting her bag.

He motioned her away from the water. "It's better if we do this on land. I don't want to burn down my favorite fishing spot." Martinez couldn't tell if he was joking or not, but sided with caution.

He led her a hundred yards through the brush to a clearing. The stack of a decent bonfire was already set up, just waiting to be lit. The old Korean man put down his pipe and kindled a fire starter, breaking life into the incipient embers before chucking it under the dry wood. He reclaimed his smoke and took a seat on a nearby log. "That will take some time. Show me what you have brought."

Martinez took a seat next to him and presented to him the mirror, still kept in its velvet bag; the blue-sigiled waterskin filled with the waters of Narcissus; and for extra measure, the nub of the Hollow Liu had pinned down with her blade at Keller's. Yi took stock of the quiet, tall woman as she laid out the components with methodical care. "You will stay and help," he declared.

"I have not been a magician very long," she warned him.

He laughed at her admission. "I don't need your expertise. I need your determination and strength. That you have practiced long and hard," he spoke with authority.

She acquiesced. "Do I need to do anything to prepare for the ritual?"

Yi tersely shook his head. "All is ready. Just waiting for the fire." He puffed his pipe and sat in silence that Martinez dared not break. As the sun set, the blaze swelled and its growing heat kept out the coming cool of night. "It is time," he announced as he reached into his robe and threw a colored powder onto the fire. The flash in her vision momentarily blinded Martinez but the sound of Yi's chants guided her back into the ritual; she summoned her will and carefully threaded it into his song.

She had no idea what he was saying or how he was able to breathe while continuously sounding an undertone, but the soaring harmonic that came through was captivating. Intermittently, he would reach into his robe and throw more things into the fire; some fragrant, some pungent, others visually stunning as they burned. At some point, he must have thrown the piece of the Hollow in the fire as the familiar stink entered her nostrils.

Martinez wasn't sure how long they had been engaged in ritual when Yi picked up the mirror and took it out of its velvet sack. He unscrewed the cap off the waterskin and started to stream the waters of Narcissus on the mirror. His cadence quickened and Martinez watched as the water started to cascade into the mirror, not over it.

Once the last drop of it was spilt, Yi's song mellowed, ramping down from its climax. He paused his chant three times, each time blowing into the mirror and creating waves in the water beyond the glass. Finally, he ended his hymn, and the crickets and crackling fire were the only chorus in the still night.

"It is done," he vowed.

"Can I ask what exactly happened?" Martinez respectfully inquired.

"I have changed the nature of the connection between the mortal realm and that outer plane," he replied. "When it is hungry, it can no longer feed here because it will never see its target."

"Like you blacked out the mirrors?"

He smiled. "Better. Whenever it peers into the mortal realm through a reflective surface, it will always see the back of the head, not the eyes."

"Huh," was all Martinez could muster. She checked her phone; it was almost midnight. She sent off a quick text to Leader and put it away, pulling out a bottle of water and another plastic bag. "You want some jerky?" Yi quietly reached in and procured a piece of dried salted meat as they stared into the flames in companionable peace.

Epilogue

Detroit, Michigan, USA
16th of August, 4:30 p.m. (GMT-4)

Huddled away in her windowless office on the fifth floor of the Salt Mine, Martinez typed away her report. Officially, the Detroit deaths were attributed to a new synthetic drug that mimicked an opiate high, untraceable by standard drug screening and causing acute respiratory failure in some. Detroit PD had all those unsolved homicides taken off their docket, and Special Agent Martinez had a feather in her cap for solving the string of deaths.

Once the imminent threat was neutralized, the Salt Mine went to work covering up the international mass incidents, which people generally did on their own according to their personal bias. Was it in a location gripped by war? It was attributed to the other side. Was it somewhere where the ruling class has been known to use extreme measures to control their populace? It was a human rights violation, plus or minus chemical warfare. Was it in a poor or undeveloped area? It was yet another humanitarian crisis that could have been prevented if the people with money cared to fix it. There was more finessing required when it came to developed democratic areas, but there was always a more believable cause than the supernatural.

All this made it significantly easier to suss out the "conspiracy nutters" talking about monsters from another realm sucking out people's souls. While the world at large ignored them, those in the know took note and assessed what level of threat they posed; generally the dangerous ones were cunning enough to keep their mouths shut.

Martinez had filed the paperwork at the FBI Detroit Field Office this morning, and she was crossing the Ts and dotting the Is on her Salt Mine report. No matter the job, one never escaped administrative work. She clicked "send," and it was done. She still had no idea how Keller got her hands on the ritual to reach the Hollow, but it had been a whole four days without mounds of corpses piling up, so she would take the partial win. It wasn't perfect, but she could honestly say if she had to do it over again, she wouldn't have done anything differently with the knowledge she'd had at the time. That was the best anyone in her line of work could hope for, but it had made her appreciate the draw of practicing divination—even the smallest finger tipping the scale to one's benefit could be vastly influential.

She stroked the soft white petals of the lone Narcissus flower that made its way back from the Magh Meall in her pocket—in for a penny, in for a pound, and it wasn't every day that work bankrolled a million in good karma. She'd thought for sure it would die and she could dry it or press it as a memento, provided of course that she didn't die first—so far, so good. When it'd persisted in living, she put it in soil in a small pot and brought it into work. It had passed through Abram's scanners without pause, and now she had a small piece of the Magh Meall with her in the depths of the earth. She couldn't be sure if it was her imagination, but the full spectrum lights seemed to shine truer since it had found its place on her desk.

Martinez shut down her computer and was gathering her things for a quiet weekend at home when a crisp knock landed on her door. She answered with her possessions in hand. "Right on time," she greeted Liu.

"I'm never late for wine," Liu unequivocally stated. "Where do you want to go?"

Martinez bobbled her head from side to side. "I promised Aloysius I would toast his grand re-opening," she suggested.

"I'll be the oldest person in there," Liu griped as they walked up the saline ramp to the elevators. She summoned the elevator with her palm.

"Yeah, but they won't know that. Asian don't raisin," Martinez quipped, holding her eye and palm to the scanners and pressing level one.

Liu was deciding how she felt about that turn of phrase on the ride up. "Not as good as 'black don't crack,' but I'll give you credit for trying."

"It's harder to rhyme 'Asian' than you think," Martinez confirmed.

"How about you make your obligatory stop at 18 is 9 and text me when you're done there. I'll find us somewhere to drink where you don't have to wear leather and wait for a DJ to drop the beat," Liu offered as they walked into the garage.

Martinez laughed. "Sounds like a plan."

*****

Deep in earth, on the twelfth floor of the Salt Mine's lower levels, the sound of gunfire, ordinance, and anguished screams echoed from the TV. Furfur reflexively scratched an itch on his thigh before unleashing more death on the electronic battlefield. He was only allowed to play his games as packaged and couldn't connect to the internet to play other people, so the challenge of this one had largely ceased. But it was just enough to pass the time.

Sometimes he would scoff at the game designers—it's like they'd never dismembered a body before and watched the splatter. After a few minutes, the Great Earl of Hell paused his game and the screams and explosions stopped. He closed his eyes and listened, probing the invisible but palpable dome of his prison with his considerable will. He was alone.

Furfur shut off the game console and the TV and positioned

the lamp behind him just so. He stared at his reflection on the otherwise dark screen and spun his will out so thinly that it was finer than spider silk. It took absolute mastery to work magic with such a delicate touch; it was much easier to hurl power with reckless abandon. As he focused, time became immaterial and lost meaning except in the counting of it—Furfur was unaware how long it took before his reflection in the screen winked back at him.

THE END

The agents of The Salt Mine will return in *Bottom Line*

Printed in Great Britain
by Amazon